"You'v...
Brew murmured

"You want to taste my lips.... Don't be afraid, sweetheart."

Carefully Meri leaned toward him. She brushed his mouth with hers and felt him shudder. Raising her hand to his cheek, she pressed her fingers against the stubble of his beard.

"Show me you trust me," he urged softly, even as his control fled.

She let the tip of her tongue slip between his lips. She had done this in her dreams a thousand times, with darkness all around and the hot silk of his tongue luring hers. Reality was a thousand times better. He tasted male and wonderful.... Meri sighed.

Brew groaned aloud. This was the sweetest contact he'd ever known—sensitive and vulnerable, petal-soft and romantic. It was the kid stuff he'd been deprived of too early in life. It was a first for the baddest guy in town....

Dear Reader,

Temptation is Harlequin's boldest, most sensuous romance series . . . a series for the 1990s! Fast-paced, humorous, adventurous, these stories are about men and women falling in love—and making the ultimate commitment.

January 1992 marked the debut of Rebels & Rogues, our yearlong salute to the Temptation hero. In these twelve exciting books—one a month—by popular authors, including Jayne Ann Krentz, Lynn Michaels and JoAnn Ross, you'll meet men like Josh—who swore *never* to play the hero. Quade—he played by his own rules. Dash—a man who'd protect the woman he loved at any cost.

Twelve rebels and rogues—men who are rough around the edges, but incredibly sexy. Men full of charm, yet ready to fight for the love of a very special woman. . . .

I hope you enjoy Rebels & Rogues, plus all the other terrific Temptation novels coming in 1992!

Warm regards,

Birgit Davis-Todd
Senior Editor

P.S. We love to hear from our readers!

The Bad Boy

ROSEANNE WILLIAMS

Harlequin Books

TORONTO • NEW YORK • LONDON
AMSTERDAM • PARIS • SYDNEY • HAMBURG
STOCKHOLM • ATHENS • TOKYO • MILAN
MADRID • WARSAW • BUDAPEST • AUCKLAND

Published July 1992

ISBN 0-373-25501-2

THE BAD BOY

1

HE WASN'T BAD TO THE BONE, but he was bad enough that it showed. Meri Whitworth took one look at him lounging, lean and long, in the end seat of the back row. It told her all she needed to know.

With or without a cause, he was a rebel, a master of misbehavior—every English teacher's nightmare. His black hair reached his shoulders; his motorcycle helmet lay at his feet. She had no doubt that somewhere under his black leather jacket, white T-shirt and tight black jeans, he had at least one tattoo. *He probably parks his Harley in his bedroom*, she mused.

He glanced at her then, and she turned her back on his insolent chrome-blue gaze to write her name on the chalkboard. Pivoting back to the students with cool poise intact, she said, "Emmett Magnusson says hello from Lake Tahoe where he broke his leg skiing yesterday. He's in the hospital there and doing well. I'm Merideth Whitworth, his substitute until he's back. I—"

"Miss—or Mrs.—Whitworth?"

Half mumble, half rumble, the interruption came from the occupant of the last row. Meri knew it would be the first of many challenges unless she met it head-on.

"Merideth will do," she said. She preferred Meri, but her full name seemed the best choice for this class of adults; her marital status was her own affair.

An irreverent smile curved his full lower lip and deepened the cleft in his chin. His eyebrows rose in sardonic appraisal as he checked out her gray tailored suit and bow-tied silk blouse. He paused at her honey-blond hair, which she'd pulled back in a sedate French braid.

His expression taunted, *Miss* Whitworth. His response was "Yo . . . Merideth."

Had his tone held even a slight concession to her authority, she'd have chalked up a point for herself. However, she detected only mockery in his voice. Meri nodded. *Politeness first,* she reminded herself firmly. She looked at the rest of the group before she smiled.

Emmett's class consisted of twenty-five students who ranged in age from twenty-one to seventy-three. Typical of residents of Berkeley, California, their racial and ethnic origins were also diverse—Asian, African American, Hispanic, Caucasian.

The common denominator was that they all had dropped out of high school and now, by their own choice, were in the adult education program, working toward a General Equivalency Diploma.

"If you're wondering about my qualifications," Meri continued, "I taught English at Turner High across town for a year. For the past three years I've been teaching at the Pacific School for Gifted Girls. I'm taking a semester off right now to write my master's thesis. Emmett's SOS came just when I needed a break from research, so here I am to take up where he left off."

She didn't add that she was subbing for Emmett because the district was short of regular substitutes—and because she owed him an emotional debt nothing could ever repay.

"The office gave me a class roster, but I'd rather you each tell me who you are and what I should know about you before we begin." Walking to the front of her desk, she sat on it with her ankles crossed and her palms braced against the edge.

The man seated directly in front of her was casually dressed, appeared to be near retirement age and was giving her a friendly, half-toothless grin. A good place to start.

"Your name, sir?"

He passed the palm of one hand over the shiny dome of his bald head. "I'm Joe Bartell, Merideth. My missus and I raised six kids and seen each of 'em through their high-school diplomas. Now that I'm retired from the oil refinery up Richmond way, it's *my* turn."

"Joe." Meri smiled, gave him a thumbs-up, then nodded to the woman behind him.

"Arlene Ainsworth," she said. "Divorced. Three children. Working a no-thanks waitressing job for a no-thanks wage. I need my GED to get a better job."

Next was Hector Chamorro, a handsome gardener whose ambition was to be the first high-school graduate in his family. Next was Mai Nguyen, a petite, soft-spoken seamstress, who hoped to become an electrical engineer.

Charleston Lamb followed—a seventy-three-year-old black man who wanted a diploma because his wife had told him that education turned her on. His flashing smile and droll delivery showed Meri she had a natural comedian in the class. Humor was always a help.

One by one, the rest introduced themselves and their aspirations. Last came the rebel.

"Brew," he said after a long silence. Then, as if it were an afterthought, he added his surname. "Brodrick."

Meri tensed. There was only one Brodrick on the class roster, first name Baxter. According to Emmett, Brodrick's work schedule allowed him to attend only one of the three night classes each week. By special arrangement, Emmett taught him at home on Friday afternoons and Sunday nights. Meri had agreed to do the same.

That was before Brew had identified himself. She'd assumed that Baxter was one of two absent students. She saw now why Emmett hadn't mentioned anything more about Baxter Brodrick, including the nickname he evidently preferred. She'd expected an older, family man of upright character and solid integrity who worked weeknights—not someone nearer her own age with an Attitude.

Certainly not this "dark Brew."

Meri gave him several moments to offer a word or two about himself, as the others had. He only stared at her. If he'd been a teenage high-school student, she'd have stared him down. She hadn't survived her year at Turner High without learning to eye wrestle. She'd only lost once. Once had been enough.

However, Brew wasn't a teenage tough. He was six feet of sexy, street-smart adult male, and Meri wasn't quite sure how to handle him. Especially when the set of his eyes and mouth told her he'd rather eat his helmet than blink an eyelid in defeat. In his case, Meri concluded, her best response might be none at all.

Out of the corner of her eye she saw Joe yawn. That made her mind up for her. As satisfying as it would have been to win this staring match, it would be a waste of everyone's time. With a shrug, she deliberately broke eye contact with Brew and launched into Emmett's lesson plan for that evening. The correct use of the pronouns *me, myself* and *I* was first on the agenda. Potentially boring, but necessary.

"Charleston," she began briskly, "would I be correct in saying, 'My daughter and myself went shopping last Saturday'?"

Charleston stroked his white mustache. "Well, now," he said, "that depends, doesn't it? First, do you have a daughter, Merideth?"

"Yes."

His hazel eyes danced. "And did you and your daughter go shopping?"

"Yes," she replied, starting to grin.

"Last Saturday?"

She posed an inquiry of her own. "Sir, are you here for GED, or a Ph.D. in courtroom interrogation?"

Everyone laughed with her. Even Brew's mouth twitched in amusement. *So Mr. Too-Cool-For-School-Until-Now isn't impervious,* she thought. It warmed her, that thought. But there was no time to analyze why.

Charleston chuckled. "Today the GED, tomorrow the California bar exam. But for right now, *was* it Saturday you went shopping?"

"Yes."

"Well, then, aside from the main facts being right, the rest was wrong. You should have said, 'My daughter and *I* went shopping last Saturday."

"Thank you at long, long last, Charleston." Meri smiled, then looked at the Vietnamese seamstress. "Is he right, Mai?"

"Quite right, ma'am."

"How can you tell?"

"Because it sounds funny to say, '*Myself* went shopping.'" Mai frowned. "Right?"

"Right. Very good." Meri looked across the room. "Brew," she forced herself to say, "if you had come along on that shopping trip, could I correctly tell the class, 'He joined my daughter and myself'?"

A moment passed, then another.

Meri was about to divert the question to another student when Brew replied, "No way."

"Why not?"

"I'm no joiner."

Meri gave him a visual once-over equal to the one he'd given her. "Stating the obvious isn't answering the question."

"Would you repeat the question, Merideth?"

"Are you prepared to answer it, Brew?"

"*I'll* answer it," Joe interceded, snapping the building tension with a total lack of guile. "You see, sayin' 'He joined my daughter and myself' ain't—I mean isn't—proper, but even slick-talk politicians on TV get grammar like that twisted up somethin' awful. But if you said, 'He joined my daughter and me,' you'd be right and that's a fact." To carry home the point, he slapped a broad, work-worn hand down on his desk.

Meri could have hugged Joe for saving her from a verbal sparring match. She hated to think she had let Brew get under her skin that much.

Obviously, the only way to avoid confrontation was to avoid asking him questions.

Meri didn't spare Brew another glance during the class hour. Finally, she said, "That's it for tonight. Hand in your spelling tests as you leave. I'll see you tomorrow night."

"Thank ya kindly," Joe said on his way out.

"Ditto," Arlene echoed, walking right behind him.

Hector handed her his test with a flourish. *"Gracias. Buenas noches."*

Meri tried unsuccessfully to recall the last time a high-school student had thanked her for anything to do with pronouns, adverbs and spelling. She'd been thanked for other things, but never for simply teaching English.

"All in all we're a decent bunch, wouldn't you say?" Charleston asked.

Meri nodded. "Emmett told me this is his best class yet. He promised I'd enjoy myself."

"Did you?"

"Very much."

Charleston glanced at Brew, who was lingering in the last row, and lowered his voice to a whisper. "He enjoyed you, too—a tad more than he'd like you to know."

Meri raised an eyebrow in disbelief.

"Oh, he's raised hell in his time," Charleston murmured. "Anyone can see that. But what hell-raiser who hasn't reformed a tad spends his nights getting his GED? Consider that."

"His classroom attitude needs more than a 'tad' of reform," Meri murmured back. "Or does he give Emmett a bad time, too?"

"Emmett? Never. But then Emmett isn't a pretty woman. Is he, now?"

Flashing her a savvy wink, Charleston added his test to the sheaf she held and limped out the door with the aid of his cane.

Meri glanced over at Brew. He stood facing her, tall and broad-shouldered. With his weight shifted onto one leg, his helmet dangling by its chin strap from his right hand, the thumb of his other hand hooked on a belt loop, he was all rogue male.

"I scare you, don't I?" he challenged, his eyes cold. He walked a straight line toward her.

Before the papers in her hand could rustle, Meri laid them down on the desk with a trembling hand.

"No," she replied, "you don't." He reminded her of her daughter's father—moody, edgy, dangerous. She wished that she'd left the room with the others.

"What scares you about me?" Stopping in front of her desk, he held up his helmet. "This?"

"No."

He unhooked his thumb from his belt loop and ran it down the open front of his black leather jacket. "This?"

"No."

"This?" He traced a diagonal scar that bisected his left eyebrow.

She clenched her jaw. "No."

"You'd be twice as freaked if you could see my tattoo," he said quietly. "You're not much of a liar."

"You're even less of a gentleman," she retorted, lifting her chin.

For just an instant, he looked stung, as if she had slapped him hard across the face. Then he smiled slowly for the first time, revealing even, white teeth.

"I'm also your tough luck, come Fridays and Sundays until Emmett's back," he countered. "Where do we meet? My place or yours?"

"As you wish, Brew."

"Mine."

"Fine. Emmett gave me the address. I'll be there on Friday at three."

"And running scared an hour later like you are now?"

"I won't be running scared, Brew."

"Who says?" he inquired. In a sudden move, he slipped his free hand beneath his jacket at his chest.

Meri caught her breath. She stepped back. An image of a switchblade knife flashed into her mind. She told herself she was overreacting, thinking he had a weapon. The past was past. Just because she'd once faced a switchblade in a classroom didn't mean she had the same thing coming from Brew. Even so, her knees began to quiver.

"You know what I can't figure?" Brew said.

She swallowed hard. "W-what?"

"Why you, a Mansfield from high-class Piedmont, taught public school for a year. You *are* Matilda Mansfield's granddaughter, aren't you?"

Meri nodded warily. "How do you know that?"

"A rocket scientist like me, you mean?"

"I didn't mean to imply that—"

"Save your excuses. I know, because newspapers helped pass the two years I spent in prison for car theft. I read every page from the obits to the society column. You were a debutante, Miss Merideth Mansfield. Looked like Princess Grace. Still do."

"That was a long time ago," she murmured. *Prison. Car theft.* She touched her tongue to her lips and kept her eyes on the spot where his hand rested under his jacket.

Brew shrugged. "It still doesn't explain you teaching school. Private girls' school, maybe. But not Turner High."

"Turner High was a long time ago, too. I taught there because the Mansfield family has a long history of public service." If explaining would stall him, she would explain ad infinitum. "My contribution wasn't as prominent as other Mansfields', but it did serve the public good."

"For one whole year," he observed, his lip curling with contempt. "Big deal. What squeezed you out? Rude dudes like me?"

Meri willed herself to meet his gaze, telling herself that he couldn't know how close to the truth he'd come. "Just like you," she confirmed, making the truth sound facetious and insincere.

Brew looked unconvinced by her reply. "You still live in Piedmont?"

"Yes. With my daughter and grandmother."

"I didn't know you got married."

"It was society column chitchat for a day."

"Still married?"

"No. My divorce was chitchat for a day, too." To prevent him from extending any cocky condolences, she asked, "How did you miss reading about both events in the papers?"

"I stopped reading the social columns after I got out of the slammer. Piedmont didn't change while I was locked up. It's posh digs for a schoolteacher, whichever way you cut it, Merideth."

"Is it my social background that irks you, Brew?"

"You bet. Same as mine ticks you off about me."

"I'm not at all—"

"You're ticked off. I saw your nose go up the minute you saw me. I saw the way you looked down at me when I was checking you out." He smiled wryly. "The debutante and the delinquent. Talk about odd couples. We're one for the books, now that Emmett's laid up."

"He'll be well soon," she said and took another careful step back.

"Not soon enough for you. You're wishing he'd paired you up with a nice, tame Yuppie instead of me." His tone was silky smooth, his eyes hard blue steel.

"*I* see no reason why we can't get along for as long as necessary, Brew."

"Stop shaking in your shoes and I'll believe it."

"I can't when you're . . ." His hand moved slightly under his jacket.

"When I'm what?"

"When you're . . ."

"Not someone you can trust?"

"I didn't say that."

"You're thinking it with every step back you take."

Meri backed up even as he accused her of doing so. His hand moved under his jacket as if to take hold of something. "If you touch me," she warned, "I'll—"

"Who says I'm going to touch?" He walked around the desk.

She lifted her head. "Don't you dare."

Step by step he closed in on her.

Meri stood her ground. "If you do I'll scream, Brew."

"Even if I don't touch?" Brew inquired. He withdrew his hand in a sharp, swift movement.

Meri sucked in a huge breath for a gargantuan scream. Air whooshed out soundlessly when she saw what he held.

"Here." He waved his spelling test under her nose. "All yours."

She stared at him, motionless, hands half lifted to ward him off, her scream dead in her throat.

He slid the folded paper between her left suit lapel and her silk blouse, then moved to the door. He paused and turned. He held her stunned gaze for a tense moment.

"What were you expecting, Merideth?" he asked. "A switchblade? Brass knuckles? Worse?"

Meri saw him leave, heard the classroom door slam, felt her heart pound. Knees buckling, she pulled her desk chair close and sank into it.

Switchblade, brass knuckles, worse....

She had faced a knife and worse at Turner High and she closed her eyes against the memories. Taking deep, calming breaths, she rocked in her chair.

Think of Trina, she repeated to herself. *Think of the good that came of the bad.* She focused on the present and on her daughter, the heart of her life.

Finally calm, she opened her eyes and added Brew's test to the others. There. Smoothing the page out on top of the pile with fingers that shook just slightly, she noted that he had misspelled the first word, committment. Three *t*'s were one too many.

She scanned the rest of his test. One wrong out of twenty. Emmett would be pleased. He always was when any student succeeded.

If anyone was born to teach, it was that rumpled, ruddy-faced, teddy bear of a man. A dedicated bachelor ten years her senior, Emmett had been her master teacher in her student-teaching days at Turner High and had gradually become a close friend. Two pleasant but sparkless dates had led them into close friendship rather than romance.

Meri checked her watch. With night classes over, the building had quieted. Time alone was nice, and useful. She wrote Brew's score on his test and graded the others, then started working out the next lesson plan.

Her encounter with Brew had stirred up old memories. She wanted to tell Emmett she'd been mistaken in agreeing to tutor Brew Brodrick, yet she couldn't.

Solid, unquestioning, Emmett had been at her side in those disastrous days four years ago. He had even offered to marry her, no questions asked, on the day she'd told him she was pregnant—even though she'd never told him the true circumstances. There was no better friend. She couldn't fail Emmett.

She stood and placed the papers in her briefcase. Removing her keys, she snapped the case shut. Would forced contact with Brew keep stirring up those buried emotions? Meri squared her shoulders. If she needed to make a greater effort than usual to hold her memories at bay, she would do it.

She walked through the empty halls of the community college, allowing her mind to wander. People said bubbly, three-year-old Trina, with gray eyes, blond curls and even features, looked just like her; and Meri had to agree that the resemblance was strong.

Trina's first spoken word had been *Mama*. The next had been *Jug*, Meri's pet name for the brown VW Beetle she had acquired in college. Meri hadn't had the heart to sell "the Jug" after recently purchasing a new car. And since the new model had just gone into the shop for transmission adjustments, the old, faithful VW had come in handy tonight.

The faculty parking area was empty except for the Jug. She glanced over at the adjacent student parking lot. A huge, black, chrome-trimmed motorcycle was the only vehicle there.

Brew Brodrick was straddling the bike, facing her way.

2

A LUMP OF FEAR FORMED in Meri's throat. Why was Brew still in the parking lot? She hurried to the Jug.

As she unlocked the door, she heard Brew's motorcycle roar to life. Steeling her spine against the sound, she slid into the driver's seat and started the Jug. The old engine sputtered to life, coughed, then died.

She locked the door from the inside and turned the key again. The motor wheezed and caught in an uneven rhythm—it always took a minute or so to warm up before it would go.

"Warm up quick, Jug," Meri whispered, pumping the gas pedal.

With the sound of Brew's bike drowned out by the VW's engine, she tried to calm herself with thoughts of Trina, but could only think of Brew on his motorcycle. Was he still out there? She hoped not. She bowed her head to the steering wheel and listened to the balky engine for the first sign that it wouldn't die if she released the clutch.

A knock sounded at her left ear. Startled, she jerked upright and saw that Brew had drawn up beside her on his black bike. He rapped again on her window with a fist gloved in black leather. His features were indistinct behind the wind guard of his helmet.

Swallowing back a gasp of alarm, she raised her eyebrows questioningly. He lifted the visor and made a circular motion with his gloved hand for her to lower her window. She rolled it down an inch and no more.

"You've got a flat," he called in above the tinny racket of the VW's motor. "Right rear."

Was the tire truly flat? Or was he saying it to lure her out of the car? She hadn't noticed a flat when she'd approached the Jug earlier, but perhaps she'd been noticing *him* in the next lot more than anything else. Getting out to check the tire would be unwise. She rolled the window up. Locked in the Jug she was safe—safer than she'd been in her classroom on the night Trina had been conceived.

But when Brew swung off his bike and set the kickstand, she felt unsafe even behind locked doors. He motioned for her to cut the Jug's motor and she hesitated. There was only one way to determine the truth without abandoning safety, she decided. Holding her breath, she revved the gas pedal, threw the gearshift into reverse, engaged the clutch and backed up.

Thunk, thunk, thunk. Meri braked and let out the breath she was holding. Flat, right rear, just as he'd said. Very observant of him to have noticed it in passing. Or had he? Was the flat his doing? She examined him through the window. Maybe not. His black brows were drawn together in a quizzical frown, his gloved hands spread, palms up. He was clearly wondering why she'd backed up on a flat rear tire—was she crazy or what?

"Not crazy," she muttered. "Just suspicious." Easy rider or biker from hell, Brew Brodrick was not someone she wanted to be alone with in an empty parking lot.

She lowered the window a bit and called out, "Would you call me a tow truck, please?"

He bent to look in at her. "Sure," he replied. "You're a tow truck, Merideth." He paused to grin wryly. "Anything else you want to be called?"

"I meant go to a phone booth and call, if you would," Meri said through clenched teeth.

"Can't hear you over the noise of your tin-can car. Speak up."

"Call a tow truck to change the tire!" she shouted, loudly enough that he pulled back a few inches.

He seemed to consider her request, then shook his head. "*I'll* change it."

"No need," she replied. "My auto insurance pays for roadside service."

"I'm all the roadside service you need." He slid the fingers of both hands into the window opening and hooked them over the glass. "Besides, you'd be alone out here if I left."

Meri looked from his invading, gloved fingers to his face. His eyes were narrowed intently on her. She felt for the window lever with her left hand and rolled it up just enough for him to feel the pinch.

"I'll take care of myself, thank you," she said.

He grimaced, then retorted, "No, you won't. And you won't break my knuckles, either."

The window lever began turning in her hand. He was forcing the window down! She tried to stop the handle from turning, first with one hand, then with both. Inexorably, the handle kept moving and the window lowered.

Night air whooshed into the Jug, carrying the smell of exhaust fumes and leather. Meri shrank back as Brew reached past her, turned the ignition off and pulled the key out.

"What's your problem with me?" he muttered into the sudden silence.

Rigid in her seat, Meri became aware that her left foot was frozen to the clutch pedal, her right to the accelerator. She was trapped and she knew it. The passenger door always stuck. There was no way out other than getting past Brew.

"Please," she said in a shaky voice. "Just go and call for me." She shivered. Her teeth began to chatter.

Brew straightened and took off his helmet. "You cold?"

She shook her head.

"Here." Brew shrugged out of his jacket. "Step out and put it on. Take advantage. I only do my white-knight bit once every blue moon."

She tried to move, to shake her head, and couldn't.

"Look, I may be bad company," Brew growled, "but this isn't. Wear it and warm up." He shoved the jacket through the open window and onto her lap, then moved to the front of the Jug and unlocked the trunk with the keys he'd taken.

Now, Meri told herself. *Break and run to somewhere safer!* She also told herself she was overreacting, but she had the door half-open before she could control the panic reflex. The Jug rocked and she looked up. Brew was lifting the spare out of the trunk. She wavered for a moment. He was only doing what he'd said he'd do. Changing the flat. Just that. Nothing more.

When she heard the clunk of the jack on the pavement, she knew for certain that she'd almost bolted and run for no reason. Sinking back into the seat, she let the door swing wide open and released a ragged sigh. What sweet relief it was to know she'd been wrong. Brew had stopped to help, not to hurt.

She touched the jacket in her lap and for the first time in years voluntarily breathed in the scent of leather— and with it, the scent of a man. With shaky legs, she slid out of the Jug and put Brew's jacket on.

Hunched over the spare, he looked up when she came around to the front of the car. "Guess what?" he asked.

"What?"

"Your spare's as flat as your flat. When was the last time you checked it out?"

"I—" Meri slid her hands into his jacket pockets "—I don't remember." She felt too embarrassed to admit that she'd *never* checked the spare, much less pumped it up.

"Don't remember," he repeated slowly. "You will after this, won't you?"

She nodded. "It appears I'll need a tow truck, after all."

Brew stood. "I can ride you home on the bike. Tomorrow you get someone to ride you back, get the spare pumped, change the tire and you got it made."

Meri glanced from him to his motorcycle. It was all black, trimmed in gleaming chrome. In flame-tipped red letters, TNT was stenciled on the sleek flank of the gas tank. The machine looked as dark and dangerous as the man who rode it.

Ride home on *that?*

Brew read her expression. *Right, Miss Piedmont. On that.* She'd look damned strange on it, too, in her prim suit and buttoned-to-the-collar blouse. Strange...and sexy all the same. But "prim" was for preppies. It had never primed his pump before, so why think twice about it right now?

Meri looked from TNT to Brew. Ride home behind *him?*

He read her again. *Yep. Behind yours truly.* He watched her glance down at the narrow skirt she wore. *Yep. With your skinny skirt pushed up and your legs wrapped around the baddest boy in school.* Brew was pretty sure what she'd say to that. She didn't let him down.

"I can't," she said. "I don't have a helmet."

He shrugged. "I'll barehead it. Use mine."

"And leave *you* unsafe? No, I'd better call a tow."

"From what phone?"

"The pay phone inside."

"Building's locked from the outside this time of night," he advised. "You have a master key?"

"No. Only a classroom key."

"Good luck."

"Where else are there pay phones around here?"

"I just used one outside the student union."

"Which is where?"

"Behind the main building. This your first time on campus?"

Glaring, she reached inside the car and pulled her purse out of her briefcase. She unzipped the change compartment and glanced up.

"Out of change?"

She nodded.

"Too bad," he said. "I don't have any to loan."

"Do you have any at all?"

"Nope. Just bills. Want a ride?"

She looked around, irritated by his nonchalance and the increasing complexity of her situation. "There must be a night watchman here or someone who can help."

"You've *got* help." He held out his helmet. "Put it on. Let's hit the road."

She gestured at her car. "I can't just leave the Jug like this."

"The what?"

"Nothing. Never mind. Would you know if there's a bus that runs from here to Piedmont?"

"Can't say. Public transportation isn't my thing." He shrugged, fighting a grin. "The Jug, eh? Good name for it. Looks like one." He dangled the helmet from his index finger. "Are you wearing this home, or what?"

"What about the Ju—er, my car?"

"Lock it up. Kiss it good-night. It'll be here in the morning." At her dubious expression, he added, "Take it from an ex-con. I know what gets stripped and stolen, and how and why. This baby won't disappear overnight."

"What are you doing here this late?" she asked warily as she took the helmet. *An ex-con!*

"After class I made a long phone call," he replied. "To a lady. Used my last quarter, or I'd have one for you.

The lady's expecting me, so let's split before I have a load of explaining to do."

Brew could see from the swift changes in her expression that Meri was making quick judgments about his "lady." Not that she was imagining him meeting a classy babe like herself, he surmised. She was picturing a tough-talkin', loose-livin' motorcycle mama. She was also figuring she had less to fear from a biker who had a date to keep.

So he'd let her think what she thought. Over the years, he'd had more than his share of wild women in leather tights with fringes flying in the wind. Blond, brunette, redhead—tall, short, in-between, the many who had caught his eye had been his companions for as long as he'd wanted them. Which wasn't long.

The urges he'd satisfied had been purely sexual. There wasn't much he hadn't learned about women in bed—what they liked and didn't like, what drove them wild.

If Merideth Whitworth wanted to picture him with a gum-snapping biker babe, she could. He wasn't going to confide that he'd outgrown his rowdy, raunchy, reckless urges for hot bodies between his sheets. It was his own business that he was choosier now than he'd been a year ago.

She didn't need to know that he'd met one special woman a year ago and discovered he was capable of love. Women were a different story for him now. Shannon was all the woman he had wanted in his life for the past year. She was a lot closer to his type than Merideth Mansfield Whitworth was.

"Do you have a nickname I could call you?" he asked on impulse.

"Why?"

"Merideth's a mouthful." He shrugged. "Like my real name is. Do I look like a Baxter to you?"

"Don't I look like a Merideth to *you?*" she returned.

She did, and then again she didn't. He scowled, annoyed at her no-answer response and at himself for asking anything so personal of a Piedmont princess.

"Forget it, Merideth. Forget I thought you might have a bite-size tag like Brew. Put the damned helmet on."

"Is Meri bite-size enough, Brew?"

"Meri's cool," he said after a flicker of surprise that she'd offered him an option, after all. Meri. It was a better fit than Merideth.

He watched Meri pull his helmet on over her sedate, blond, French braid. Shannon sometimes wore hers in the same style. Unlike Meri, Shannon was brunette, and shorter, smaller, sassier. Meri's eyes were gray, Shannon's were blue. Chrome blue, Shannon liked to say. In a year of living with her, Brew had discovered that love could change a guy—even a guy who had a past and an attitude to match.

"It's kind of you to go out of your way," Meri said. Brew put the spare and her briefcase in the trunk and locked the Jug's door. "I appreciate your help."

"You'd better," he replied brusquely. "Not so long ago I'd have left you to fend for yourself."

"Well, thank you just the same."

"You're welcome just the same."

She slung her purse over her shoulder, then fumbled with the helmet strap under her chin.

"Need a hand with that?"

She backed away. "No. I can manage it."

"You're managing it wrong," he said, stepping up to her. He closed his fingers over hers and found them cold to the touch, her palms clammy. Brew knew fear when he saw it. She was scared.

Why? Because he was a man and she was a woman, and every female had something to fear from the opposite sex? Maybe. Or maybe because he was an ex-con biker and she was a social-register blue blood.

What was she like when she felt safe and warm with a man? Brew wondered. What sort of man would turn her on? Not a biker. Uh-uh. She looked ready to back away again because he'd invaded her personal space.

He let her hands go and felt a small, unexplainable loss in his gut as he did. He fastened the strap quickly. The skin of her throat felt silk-smooth under his fingertips. He had an urge to slide them down to the top button of her collar. Before Shannon, he'd have done it. Oh, yeah, he'd have tested even a Mansfield for any hidden interest in him. He didn't now, not anymore. He checked the impulse.

It still enraged Brew to think of any man testing Shannon like that. He'd break the guy's neck, and the rest of his anatomy for good measure. Besides, Meri might have a man who'd see red, too, if he found out she'd been felt up in the faculty parking lot. What sort of man would she have? Probably a pencil neck in a designer suit who didn't know a switchblade from a letter opener. *A real threat*, he thought. Even so, Brew turned away from temptation, mounted his bike and started it.

"Hitch up your skirt and hop on," he called over the roar of the motor. She failed to make a convincing move, so he checked out her long-legged, small-breasted figure and lied. "I'm not big on legs. D cups ring my doorbell. You're safe both ways. Get on."

When Meri hitched her skirt up, Brew rated her legs fifteen on a scale of ten. He wondered if she knew how to use them, then stopped himself. Scoping women, rating them, mentally undressing them had all been reflex before Shannon. He puffed out a quick breath as Meri settled behind him on the bike. High heels and panty hose. No slip, though.

He liked the idea of slips—lacy ones that made see-through patterns against creamy skin and small breasts like Meri's. He puffed out another little breath. Keeping Shannon foremost in his mind might be a little harder tonight than usual.

"This your first hog ride?" he inquired even though he could tell from the way she was sitting behind him that it was. He figured it was best to make one crude stab at polite conversation before he manhandled her eye-popping legs into position and ordered her to hug him tight.

"What kind of ride?"

"Bike. Chopper. Hog."

"Oh . . . yes, my first."

"Uh-huh. Well, it's all a matter of balance," he informed her. "We've got to be in sync, you see—like one rider instead of two. Scoot forward."

She scooted, but not by the necessary margin.

He craned his head around. "Closer. Hips against mine. Legs against mine. One body. Got it?"

Brew felt it when she got it. A perfect fit. That hadn't happened often with his former passengers. He felt her catchy gasp in his ear as he slid his right hand down the outside of her right calf and closed his fingers around her ankle. She tensed at his touch.

"Relax," he commanded. He guided her instep to the foot peg on that side. "Now the left one." He let her place that foot securely on the opposite peg without his help because the feel of her leg against his hand had given him a real charge. He hadn't bargained on that.

Sure, she had great legs, but hers weren't the first great legs he'd ridden between in his life. So why was there something unique about the feel of her against him?

"Great," he said. "Now hug your arms around me tight." He felt her fumble instead with something behind him. "What are you doing?"

"Zipping this jacket up."

"Forget that. Zipper broke last week. Lay it open, make friends with my back and hold on like you mean it."

When she didn't move after a couple of seconds, he knew she'd need prompting.

"Listen," he said over his shoulder. "Riding in just my T-shirt I'll need all the body heat I can get. And no, I won't take my jacket back, so keep it to yourself."

"Perfect," he said when she finally came flush against his back and her arms circled his ribs. He clenched his stomach muscles as her palms flattened hesitantly against them. He felt the chill of her fingers through his T-shirt, then felt a surge of male heat below his belt buckle.

He had to wonder then why he'd thought getting her home would be simple. There was nothing simple about the mold of her body to his. Here he was, a man who had carted the wildest of women around on his bike, yet no female had ever affected him like Miss Prim was doing.

It made no sense, he told himself. Zip. Zero. Zilch. There was no way he'd expected his jeans to be so tight all of a sudden.

"Lean when I lean," he told her, and they took off.

Meri squeezed her eyes shut and held on even tighter. What, she asked herself, was the charm of total exposure to the open road for people like Brew? With all the trains, boats, planes and cars in the world, who needed this life-threatening mode of travel? She opened her eyes just enough for a peek through the visor at the pavement. Dizzy, she shut them again. She didn't want to watch the black asphalt hurling by, just inches from her feet.

Here she was, flying through the night on a machine whose engine power, even at moderate speed, vibrated nonstop through her body. Here she was with her legs bared to the tops of her thighs, glued to Brew Brodrick like a needy lover. Or a greedy one. No doubt he'd had hordes of both.

She felt the hard plane of his stomach under her palms. His long, wind-whipped black hair lashed her lower face and throat. Reflexively, she clung more tightly to him. This dark brew of a male was her only solid point of reference in a night that was tilting to reality's far side. He was so big, so strong. She hadn't been this close to a man's body since—

Stop. She wouldn't think of that. She'd think of something else. She visualized Gran tucking Trina into bed. It was a soothing image, except that Gran had probably not read Trina a bedtime story and was lecturing instead: "Public service is a Mansfield tradition, Katrina, dear."

Every Mansfield was expected to uphold so many traditions. Meri could recite them in her sleep. Mansfields were never freethinkers, dilettantes or free spirits, except for Curtis, Jr., her father. He'd caused the only scandal in the family and had died tragically with her mother in his early twenties.

Gran had taken Meri in and brought her up in the family tradition. And Meri was grateful, but still wasn't certain that Gran felt more than a perfunctory affection for her. She could count on both hands the number of hugs and kisses Gran had given her in her life.

However, Gran was demonstrative with no one, Meri reminded herself. Gran had been convent educated and strictly brought up in the highest, most straitlaced enclave of Boston society. After numerous Easter vacations spent with Gran's relatives in Boston, Meri knew what compelling forces had shaped Gran's narrow viewpoint and upright character.

Gran would be horrified to see her now, speeding through the night with Brew Brodrick on his bike.

Meri suddenly wondered what brand of shampoo Brew used. His hair smelled good—wonderful—like whatever made her favorite tea, Earl Grey smell so unlike tea. Bergamot. That was it. Was it an herb or a spice or...?

She opened her eyes as Brew slowed and braked at a stoplight. They were in an unfamiliar industrial area of Berkeley. The bike was the only vehicle at the intersection.

"Where are we?"

"Where people like me work and live," Brew replied. "I took a shortcut."

Meri glanced around at the dark-windowed warehouses and small factories on either side. Only half the streetlights shone in the lower-income neighborhood. The dimly lit street seemed threatening, and she resisted the urge to hug Brew even tighter.

"What work do you do here?" she asked to distract herself.

"Motorcycle detailing. Old bikes, mostly. Antiques. A friend of mine runs the shop. I live in the apartment above it." He shifted in the circle of her arms. "How ya doin' back there?"

"I'm...okay." She couldn't say "Just fine" and mean it. She pulled back a little from her hold on Brew. A shortcut? To Piedmont? There were no street signs marking any of the four corners in this dark side of town. She couldn't tell where she was. Apprehensive, she wished she'd kept her eyes open.

Then, suddenly, a motorcycle thundered through the intersection at high speed, a young blond male and a dark-haired female astride. Definitely over the speed limit. Neither rider wore a helmet.

"Damn!" Brew exclaimed. Revving into gear, he yelled back at her, "I have a score to settle with those two. Hold on."

Meri had no choice but to reclaim her bear hug on him. He burned rubber on takeoff. *A score to settle.* She vowed that the minute he stopped, she'd get off the bike and refuse to ride one inch farther.

She kept an eye out for a bus stop and saw one on the left as they whizzed past. Waiting for a bus late at night had to be safer than getting tangled up with Brew Brodrick in a street brawl.

Within a couple of blocks, Brew came abreast of the other bike. The riders looked over. The boy's eyes widened when he recognized Brew. The girl was wearing sunglasses. Brew was going to settle a score with teenagers?

He said nothing, just pointed right. Paling, the boy pulled to a screeching halt at the curb. Brew parked behind them and got off his bike. They stayed on theirs, the boy staring at Brew as he approached.

"Brew," the girl began nervously, "I was just—"

"I know what you were just," Brew gruffly cut in. "I wasn't born last night, babe."

Meri recognized her golden moment to slide off the bike and backtrack to the bus stop. But how could she abandon two teens to Brew?

"C'mon, Brew," the girl protested. "Give me a break."

"Can it, Shannon," Brew snapped. "You said you'd head straight home from work on the bus when I called you from school. If that's a bus, I'm the Pope."

"Brew, you never understand. You—"

"I understand plenty. This is the last time you cheat on me, lady."

Cheat? Meri's mind raced. He'd said earlier, "The lady's expecting me." This was the lady? This girl?

Glaring at the boy, Brew added, "And you'll sing soprano for life if you raid my roost again. You got that, Duke?"

"Yeah, Brew," Duke muttered sullenly. "Sure."

"Don't forget it on the road home." Brew glared at Shannon. "You'll burn good when I get there. First for cheating me with him and next for biking bareheaded. In the meantime, I have a delivery to make." He hiked a thumb in Meri's direction.

Meri removed her helmet, aghast at what she'd heard. This girl—this *child*—was cheating on Brew? Did Emmett know Brew had an underage girlfriend?

She couldn't imagine Emmett knowing and doing nothing about it. He couldn't possibly know. She was going to confront Brew about preferring girls to women. And about picking fights with kids.

"Who's she?" Shannon asked.

"She's Emmett for the next few weeks. Now, get this lady home, Duke. Go steal yourself someone else's girl."

Duke and Shannon drove off in a cloud of exhaust.

Brew turned to Meri. "She's more than I can handle half of the time," he said. "Sorry."

Meri pictured Trina being misused in her teen years. A fierce, protective urge rose in her at the thought. Adrenaline followed instinct. Meri's desire to break and run was gone. Now she wanted to rake Brew over the coals.

"You should be more than just sorry," she said furiously, hauling herself off the bike to face him.

"For what? Why?"

"Shannon can't be more than sixteen."

"Fifteen," he corrected. "Old enough to work one night a week at a doughnut shop. *And* old enough to know better than to cross me."

"You should be ashamed."

Brew shrugged. "When I get home I'll straighten her out."

"With what?" Meri demanded. "Your fists . . . or worse?"

He blinked and backed up a step as she closed in on him. "You think I'd beat that sweet young thing for cheating me with Duke Doyle?"

Meri snapped, "I don't put anything past you after what I've just heard. Surely you realize you could be arrested and jailed."

"For what?" He halted.

She glowered at him. "For misusing an underage girl—or worse, from the sound of it."

He didn't reply for a long moment, then comprehension registered. "You should teach math instead of grammar, Meri," he advised coldly. "You add one and one real fast. Biker plus jailbait equals just what people like you expect of me, doesn't it?"

"I didn't expect this."

"Way down low you did," he said in a hard, level tone. "I know the look in your eye. I've seen it before when I've been accused of underhanded things. Some of them I did, some I didn't. But one thing I never do is 'misuse' what's mine."

"What's *yours?*" Meri retorted in disbelief. "Shannon isn't your personal property."

"She's mine to keep in line as I see fit," he shot back. "She came to me of her own free will and she stays of her own free will."

"Willing or otherwise, she's a minor, a child."

"And since she is, I must be a child molester," he mockingly rejoined. "That's what you're thinking but not saying out loud, isn't it?"

"Can you say you're anything else, Brew?"

"Yeah. I'm Shannon's father."

3

"SHANNON'S *WHAT*?" Meri stared at Brew.

"You heard me. Behind the sunglasses, she has my eyes. No mistaking whose kid she is when you see them."

"I . . ." She floundered. "I'm . . ."

"You'd better be sorry." He raised his eyebrows.

Meri took a deep breath. "I am. Very sorry that I jumped to the wrong conclusion."

"You've been doing that all night," Brew said, then looked in the direction Duke and Shannon had gone. "You've been right for the most part. I'm no Hell's Angel, but I've come close." He looked back at Meri. "I'm thirty-two years old. Shannon's fifteen, like I said. Her mom was the last of seven foster mothers I had when I was a stupid, mixed-up kid. But that's another story.

"I didn't know I was a dad until Shannon showed up a year ago. Since then, I've been a father." He paused, then added with testy emphasis, "And a damn good one. You got that?"

"Yes, Brew. I wouldn't want my daughter out late with Duke, either."

"You wouldn't want her with him, period, if you knew him. I know him. He's me when I was his age. Trouble on two wheels and looking for more." He squinted at her. "How long have you had a kid?"

"Trina's three."

"Give her twelve more years." Brew grinned ruefully. "You don't know what you're missing, Meri."

"I have a vague idea. I teach girls who are Shannon's age, remember?"

"Not *D* students like Shannon. You teach the cream of the crop. In private school, to boot."

"That doesn't mean I don't know teenagers," Meri replied, bristling a little.

"You don't know any like the one I once was, Meri. I saw that first thing tonight when class started. You still look like you're not sure what I'll do next."

"What you'll do next is take me home, Brew," she said, putting the helmet back on her head.

He stepped close as she fumbled with the chin strap. "Don't order me around outside of class, teach," he muttered. He pushed her hands away and grasped the strap. "And stop shaking every time I come close. I'm not in my attack mode tonight, okay?"

"I'm not shaking." Meri swallowed, feeling her knees tremble. He'd been wrong. She did know kids like him. One had fathered her child. He hadn't driven a motorcycle. He'd worn studded black leather, though, and the tricolor forearm tattoo of an East Bay street gang. He'd also carried a switchblade.

"What freaks you out about me?" Brew demanded. "The bike, the hair, the knife scar, what?"

Meri looked away. "Nothing."

"It's more than nothing. How are you going to teach me one-on-one come Fridays and Sundays?" He tilted her chin up and looked into her eyes. "Hmm? How, if you're so damned scared?"

Meri felt her chin quiver against his thumb, knew he felt the tremor. He was so big up close and face-to-face. So tall and muscled and power packed.

"I'll get over it by Friday," she managed to say.

"Over what?"

"Whatever it is."

"Do all bikers scare you? Is that it?"

"It may be." She turned her face to evade his touch. "A lot of people are frightened of bikers with good reason."

"Not like you've been all night," he softly accused, coasting his thumb over her lower lip. "What's the story with you, Meri? Is it me? Or is it all men? Some guy roughed you up?"

Unable to back away with Brew gripping the helmet strap, Meri shook her head.

Brew loosened his grip on the strap. She'd been more than roughed up, he decided. His instincts whispered rape. He hoped he was wrong.

"Okay." He fastened the helmet and let her go. "Your business is your business. And Fridays and Sundays are *your* problem. You sure you want to shiver and shake at *my* place?"

"My place would be best, on second thought," Meri said, backing up two steps. She didn't want it to show, but she was relieved that he hadn't insisted on meeting at his place, glad he'd offered the change.

"Yours, then," Brew agreed. "I may have to come later, around seven, so I can bring Shannon along and keep her in line. I'm grounding her for the next week. Maybe for the next month. Her grades are the pits."

"Seven's fine. Let's be on our way, shall we?"

Brew mounted the bike and motioned her onto it. Meri screwed up her courage, pulled her skirt thigh-high and got on behind him. This time she didn't hesitate to plaster herself indecently against the rear pockets of Brew's black jeans and the back of his T-shirt.

Brew took off as soon as Meri settled in behind him. She kept her eyes open and reoriented herself as he drove from Berkeley into Oakland. Knowing she was getting closer to home helped her feel safer. Knowing Brew was a protective father was reassuring.

Less calming was the knowledge that he had fathered a child at seventeen—perhaps even at fifteen. And how had he gotten involved sexually with a foster parent?

At fifteen, Meri hadn't even been kissed, much less had sex. Her first kiss at sixteen had been wet, slimy, disgusting. She had balked at kissing anyone again until the following year, when she fell in love with Harriman de Wilde III.

Harriman had known all about kissing. And petting. And making love. He'd been a year older, and light-years of dating experience ahead of her. She'd given herself to him on the night of her society debut.

They'd made fervent and furtive love that night and during the three months before he'd gone off to Princeton. Two months later, at Thanksgiving break, he'd breezed back to California with a brunette from Vassar.

Meri rolled her eyes, remembering the heartbroken but staunch vow she'd made then to never love again. It had lasted for three years until a perfectly charming, sophisticated attaché to a foreign embassy in Boston made the final semester of her senior year at college quite enlightening and memorable.

However, his return to his country—and the wife and daughter he'd neglected to mention—had been the end of that.

He'd been her last lover. Two heartbreaks had put her on guard against a third. She had dated after that, but hadn't surrendered her heart or body again.

Then there had been Trina's father.

Suppressing the flash of painful memory, she forced her thoughts back to the man in her arms. A father at seventeen. Shannon's father. Brew had survived the battleground of his troubled youth. Unlike Trina's father, Brew was alive.

Meri directed Brew through exclusive upper Piedmont to Matilda's estate, where she and Trina lived.

Brew pulled into the night-lit, semicircular drive and cut the motor. He spent a moment taking in the spacious lawns and imposing facade of Matilda's enormous house.

"I've been stuck in state reform schools smaller than where you live," he drawled over his shoulder.

"That's my grandmother's home," Meri said, dismounting. "I rent the carriage house for myself and Trina. Gran's a widow in her seventies now and prefers having us close."

"Why? So she can keep an eye on you?"

Surprised that he had guessed the truth, Meri nodded. "She fears I'll stray from the family fold as my father did. I won't, of course."

"No way," Brew agreed, flicking a glance of appraisal at her. "You're too straight." He looked away. "How did your dad stray?"

"You don't know? I thought it was public knowledge."

"Do I look like John Q. Public?" Brew retorted. "Back when I read the social columns, I never ran across why you lived with your grandmother. Fill me in, okay?"

"Okay." She matched his flip, irreverent tone. He could dish it out, but could he take it? "My father rebelled in his last year at Harvard. It was the late sixties, the peak of the surfing craze. He dropped out of college and society, became a beach-bum surfer and married a beach bunny."

Meri paused, feeling the familiar heartache of having no memory of her parents. "He and my mother, Taffy, drowned in a surfing accident at Half Moon Bay when I was six months old."

"My condolences," Brew muttered. "I bike down there every now and then to catch the sunset. Hell of an undertow there."

"Yes. They weren't the first to drown in that surf. You see why Gran's overly protective."

Brew shrugged. "I'm getting the picture." He looked around. "So here's where I'll come on Fridays and Sundays to learn my p's and q's. Where's the part you rent?"

"It's a separate building around to the side."

"I'll walk you there."

"That isn't necessary."

"I'll walk you there, Merideth."

Annoyed at his refusal to yield, Meri led him to the left of the big house. She prayed that Gran hadn't heard the bike. Ingrid, Gran's housekeeper, surely hadn't. Unlike Gran, Ingrid didn't hear well. Meri hoped they were both engrossed in watching their favorite prime-time soap opera, with the TV volume turned up for Ingrid's benefit.

"Why are you tiptoeing?" Brew asked behind her.

She almost stumbled. "Am I?"

"Yeah, you are."

She tried to walk normally without clicking her heels on the flagstone walkway. "Be careful of the stone steps ahead," she advised, so he'd watch his own feet instead.

As they rounded the corner, she saw lights on in the second-story den where Gran and Ingrid always watched *Harbor Crest*. Relieved, Meri led Brew to her snug little two-bedroom house. The porch light was lit, but it was dark inside, as she had left it. She shrugged out of Brew's jacket at the door and handed it to him with his helmet.

"Thank you again for your help," she said.

"No problem," he replied, studying her dark windows. "I'll be back around seven on Friday—with Shannon."

"I'll be expecting you. Good night."

He didn't reply or move to leave. "Your little girl's in there in the dark?" he asked.

"Oh...no. Trina goes to Gran's house on the rare evenings I'm gone. Gran and the housekeeper baby-sit and put Trina to sleep. I move her to her own bed later."

"Good. I didn't like thinking you'd leave your kid alone while you were out."

"I dislike your thinking I'd do that," she reproved.

Brew lifted one eyebrow. "You imagined worse of *me* tonight."

"When you pointed out my mistake, I apologized."

"Sorry I got the wrong idea." He added gruffly, "That puts the apologies even." He slung his jacket over his shoulder. "Is your grandmother overly protective of Trina, too?"

Meri nodded. "Trina got a bedtime story tonight if Ingrid tucked her in. If Gran tucked her in, she received a lesson in how to be a proper Mansfield."

"Some fun," he said, looking surprised. "I figured being a Mansfield was a bed of roses. Or is Gran the only thorn?"

Meri felt guilty for sounding critical. "Gran is strict, stern at times, and highly principled. I respect her very much. She gave me a proper home, upbringing and education."

"Lucky you."

Uncertain whether he was mocking or not, Meri stepped inside. "Good night."

"See you Friday," he said, and walked away.

She closed the door, switched on a lamp and stood inside wondering why she'd filled Brew in on so much of her life. Tense, she waited for the roar of Brew's bike. Seconds passed, then added up to a full minute. Clenching her hands, she marched out to investigate.

Rounding the corner of Matilda's house, she stopped short. Brew was walking his bike down the long drive. Had the engine failed? She hurried across the dew-damp lawn to him.

"What's wrong?"

He put a finger to his lips. "I don't want to wake Trina up if she's asleep."

Openmouthed, Meri stood and watched him roll the bike the rest of the way down the drive and onto the street. There, he was quickly hidden from view by the high front hedges of Matilda's grounds and those next door. Meri waited, listening for him to start up. The sound came from more than halfway down the block.

Walking back to the carriage house, she revised her first impression of Brew Brodrick.

THE NEXT MORNING AT breakfast with her grandmother and Trina in Matilda's solarium, Meri said, "I'll be tutoring one of Emmett's night students at my house twice a week, Gran." She took a sip of coffee before adding, "The student who kindly gave me a ride home last night."

"That's good of you, Merideth," Matilda commented, looking up from the morning newspaper. "Ingrid can watch Katrina if you like."

"Don't *want* Ingrid to watch me," Trina objected, pushing her lower lip out. "Want to see Mommy tutor."

"Little girls speak when spoken to and not before." Matilda lowered the half-lens reading glasses perched on her nose and gave her great-granddaughter a look of stern reproof.

Trina looked at her mother imploringly. Meri diplomatically replied, "Mind your manners for Great-Gran, sweetheart. We'll see what we can work out."

Mollified, Matilda returned to reading the morning news, Trina to the toast and jam on her plate. Meri sipped her coffee, glancing from her blond, gray-eyed daughter to her imperious, aristocratic, silver-haired grandmother.

The two were alike—strong-minded and strong-willed; far stronger in those characteristics than Meri considered herself to be. In fact, she often mediated their inevitable clashes.

Closing her eyes for a moment, Meri basked in the morning sunshine warming the Victorian solarium. She savored the deep, rich taste of coffee on her tongue. Matilda's Spanish cook had a magic touch with coffee. And he always served a dark brew.

Meri opened her eyes. She would have to explain Brew Brodrick to Matilda before Friday. Last night she hadn't revealed every detail of how she had gotten home. She had only told her about the Jug's flat tires and that one of Emmett's students had offered a ride.

Matilda had been too engrossed in *Harbor Crest* to pay close attention. Meri studied her grandmother, wondering how to announce that a long-haired, leather-jacketed biker would be learning English grammar in the carriage house twice a week.

"About this student I'll be teaching..." she ventured.

Matilda didn't look up from the Dow-Jones average. "Hmm?"

"He's...unconventional."

"What's uncovenshul, Great-Gran?" Trina piped up.

"Out of the ordinary," Matilda answered briskly, looking up over her glasses first at Trina and then at Meri. "What do you mean by unconventional, Merideth? A hippie or some such character?"

"No . . . More of a . . . motorcycle buff."

Matilda considered that. "So was dear, departed Malcolm Forbes," she granted. "Just for fun, naturally."

"Baxter Brodrick is a little younger than the late Mr. Forbes, Gran."

"As long as he isn't one of those dreadful Devil's Advocates or whatever fiendish name that rabble of a motorcycle gang goes by, Merideth, I see no cause for concern."

"He isn't," Meri replied, prudently saying no more. Though Brew was closer to Devil's Advocate than Harvard graduate, he wasn't quite "dreadful." Difficult and defiant, yes, as well as discourteous at times. But the man who had walked his bike away from the house to avoid waking a sleeping child wasn't dreadful.

It didn't describe his appearance, either. He had, after all, been clean and clean-shaven. She thought of comparing him to the late James Dean for her grandmother's benefit, but didn't. Matilda had come from a long, distinguished line of Boston blue bloods into marriage with Curtis Mansfield, Sr. An aristocrat to the core, she spared no respect for Hollywood. She wouldn't appreciate the moody bad-boy movie legend. It was even harder for Meri to imagine her grandmother approving of Brew or TNT.

"What will your schedule be with your student?" Matilda asked, scanning the society column.

"Friday and Sunday evenings."

Matilda looked up, frowning. "Weekend evenings? Why on earth?"

"Emmett says his job interferes with every weeknight but Monday."

"Job? What sort of job does the man have?"

"Emmett didn't say," Meri hedged, since she wasn't sure what motorcycle detailing actually involved.

"It won't interfere with Sunday tea, will it? I do dislike rescheduling tea, Merideth."

Meri didn't sigh, though she wished she could. It was Trina who sighed, long and loud. "Tea, tea, tea," she chanted, pulling a long face. "Who likes tea? *I* don't."

"You will when you're grown up, Katrina," Matilda said.

"Tea is the most civilized of beverages. Teatime is the most civilized hour of the day."

Meri knew from lifelong experience what Matilda would say next.

"Sunday tea is a Mansfield tradition." She looked at Meri. "Perhaps your student would enjoy taking tea with us this one time?"

"Oh, no. No," Meri hastened to repeat. "He has a— a daughter to care for, you see. He'd be too busy, I'm sure."

"No harm in being charitable on occasion, Merideth. Mansfields have obligations, remember, to those less fortunate—high-school dropouts, as well."

Meri checked her watch and quickly stood up to cut the Mansfield lecture short. "I have a lot of thesis research to do at the library today."

"Don't fret about the poor crippled Jug," Matilda said, waving a benevolent hand. "I've dispatched Lars and Santiago to fix the tires and bring it home."

"Thank you, Gran. And thank you for letting me use your Mercedes sedan today." Bending, Meri gave her grandmother a grateful kiss on one cheek. She kissed Trina on both cheeks. "Bye-bye, sweetheart. Be good to Great-Gran and Ingrid until I get back."

"I will, Mommy." Trina smiled impishly.

Driving to the library, Meri thought about Brew. She had dreamed about him last night. Fragments came back to her. His chrome-blue eyes holding her gaze... his fingers untying the satin ribbons of her eyelet-lace nightgown...his long black hair grazing the skin of her bare breasts as he bent his head to kiss them...

It had all felt so good in the dream—so good. Meri frowned. How had she dreamed of being intimate with Brew? She hadn't dreamed of sex at all since the rape, not that she could remember.

Her counselor had said that dreams of pleasurable sex, and feelings of positive attraction to a man would be a strong sign of recovery from the trauma. "You'll be hesitant when sexual feelings arise, of course, but allow yourself to feel as much as you can when they first begin," Grace Dickens had advised.

Meri had never doubted that it was sound advice, but she hadn't any reason to reflect on it until now. She shook her head. How had she ever dreamed of receiving tender, erotic pleasure from a tough bad-boy type like Brew? She associated him more with Trina's father than with the two lovers with whom she'd known pleasure.

She stilled the inner trembling she always experienced when she thought of the student who had raped her. It wasn't necessary to dwell on him, she assured herself. Even so, a distorted image of the young man's pale, angry face flooded her mind. *Stop! Stop! Stop!* she had begged during the entire ordeal.

Shaken, Meri pulled out of the traffic and parked at the curb. She told herself that she was overreacting to reminders of her experience just as she had panicked last night. Brew had unknowingly stirred her memories. There was no danger. The past would all be laid to rest again, as soon as Emmett returned.

Nonetheless, she now regretted not having told Emmett that she'd been raped by a Turner High student. Had he known, he'd *never* have asked her to fill in for him with a pupil like Brew. She'd be spending her Friday and Sunday evenings with Trina as usual, instead of with Brew; and she wouldn't be parked here, trying to calm her anxieties.

But she hadn't told him. She hadn't told anyone until she'd discovered she was pregnant. Stressed to the breaking point, she had gone to Matilda and revealed her awful secret: that she had been overpowered at knifepoint by an itinerant student she'd been trying to help at Turner High, the leader of an inner-city street gang; and that he had been stabbed to death by a rival gang shortly after the rape.

"We *will* rise above this tragedy, Merideth," she remembered Matilda intoning after a long, grim silence, "if we agree that nothing is to be gained from filing rape charges against a dead person."

"Yes, Gran. There would be no point."

"Very well, then. You, the child and the family name must be preserved from scandal. Dry your eyes. We have plans to make."

Morally and spiritually opposed to abortion—a view Meri shared—Matilda had masterminded a cover-up. She had arranged Meri's false marriage to, and divorce from, a fictitious Englishman named Alistair Whitworth.

Meri had clung to her maternal right to give her child up for adoption at birth. She had been stunned at Matilda's strenuous objection to adoption.

"That child is *half you* and therefore part Mansfield," she remembered Matilda saying. "Whereas your own faulty judgment contributed to your misfortune, the child is as innocent of blame as you were when you came into my care as an infant. I disapproved of your parents, but took responsibility for you as my own. I expect you to do the same."

After Matilda had elicited Meri's promise that no one else would be told the truth of her child's paternal origins, Meri had gone into seclusion in England where Matilda had arranged every detail of her stay, her medical care, and therapy.

Meri had fond memories of her rape counselor. Grace Dickens had been skilled, discreet and effective in leading her through stage after stage of crisis and recovery. Grace had been her mainstay and lifeline in the three months before the moment Meri felt the miracle of life move in her womb for the first time.

Meri closed her eyes and relived that miraculous moment. Love, unreasoning and profound, had flooded her world of darkness. From that instant on, adoption had been out of the question.

Half you. How wise Matilda had been. How innocent and beautiful Katrina Whitworth had been on the unforgettable day of her birth. What love she had inspired in Meri!

Composure restored, Meri steered the Mercedes away from the curb with a steadier hand. She might be the only Mansfield with a skeleton in her closet, she reflected, but only Gran would ever know it.

4

MERI GOT A PHONE CALL from Emmett on Friday morning.

"Well?" he prompted, after informing her that his leg was in traction and every nurse in the hospital was madly in love with him. "How did your week go with my twenty-five shining stars?"

"Like clockwork, Emmett. The class practically teaches itself—they're so committed to doing well. Last night Charleston had us all laughing so hard we were falling out of our seats."

Emmett chuckled. "He's a card, for sure." He paused. "And what did you think of Brew on Monday night?"

"I think you could have told me more about *Baxter* than you did at the beginning," she chided, shifting in her chair.

"I didn't want to prejudice you one way or the other," he said. "What do you think, now that you've met him?"

"He's . . ." She couldn't say that she thought of Brew entirely too often every day. As for the dreams she'd been having about him every night . . . "He's . . ."

"An experience?"

Relieved that Emmett had supplied so diplomatic a description, Meri granted, "That's one way of putting it." Then she confessed, "I'm afraid he and I got off on the wrong foot with each other at the very start. But it was temporary, I hope. I want to do well for you, Emmett, with each one of your students."

"You will," Emmett reassured her. "As Brew would say, 'Don't sweat it.' Think of him as a rough diamond, because he is. There's nothing he doesn't know about bikes, for one thing. And beer, for another. That's how he got the name, you know. Did I tell you he— Hold the phone for a sec, Meri. A gorgeous nurse just walked in with a familiar gleam in her eye."

Meri heard muffled sounds as Emmett apparently covered the receiver with his hand. She tried to picture Brew as a rough diamond. The bikes and the beer kept edging into the picture frame.

Nothing he doesn't know about bikes, she thought, remembering the flaming TNT on his motorcycle.

Nothing he doesn't know about beer, she thought, and pictured him popping metal caps off brown bottles with a flick of his thumbnail.

"Meri," said Emmett, coming back on the line, "it's my morning bath time. Catch you later. Call if you need help with lesson plans or with Brew. Bye."

Meri hung up and looked around her living room, trying to imagine the bike-and-beer expert sprawled on her camelback sofa.

Help with lesson plans? No. Help with Brew? She needed more than help. She needed to talk to her rape counselor in London who had become a close friend since her therapy. Picking up the receiver again, she pressed the memory button for Grace Dickens's number.

"Meri! It seems like ages," Grace answered. "Two long weeks, if I'm right, since we last chatted. You sound troubled. By what?"

"Dreams, Gracie. Erotic dreams."

"Splendid! You know that means you're making progress, don't you? How do you feel about them?"

"Disturbed. All mixed-up."

"Is there pleasure in these dreams?"

"Yes, but I'm so confused by it all. You know I haven't gotten involved with anyone, haven't even dated in all this time. Why erotic dreams, suddenly?"

"Hmm. Is your dream lover at all familiar to you?"

"Yes. He's an adult student of mine in a special class."

"And your dreams indicate you're feeling attracted to him," Grace surmised. "I think it's splendid. You're regaining your emotional freedom, so to speak."

"What do I do about it?" Meri groaned. "What if he . . . I'll be teaching him in private sessions for several days, and what if he . . ." She closed her eyes and shook her head.

"Meri, do you fear him?"

"Yes, and no."

"Is your fear valid?"

"Maybe not. He's spent time in prison and had a troubled youth, but Emmett arranged the private sessions. I'm sure he wouldn't have arranged them if Brew was violent or dangerous."

"His name is Brew? My, how evocative. Is he as hunky as the name suggests?"

"Gracie, you sound positively sex-starved. Alec must be out of town on business again," Meri teased.

"He is, unfortunately. Brew's name is quite a stimulus to the imagination."

Meri laughed. "You're supposed to be helping me sort through my confusion," she chided. "Be serious."

"Very well. Has the man in question given you any reason to trust him?"

Meri thought of the Jug's flat, the bike ride, and Brew's concern for Shannon. "Yes. He's also stable enough to hold down more than one job."

"Is he interested in you?"

"I'm not sure," she slowly replied. Then, in a rush, she added, "I'm so afraid I'll freak out if he *is* interested. What if he makes a move on me and I panic?"

"Meri, as you Yanks say, think positive. Rely on the good memories you have of your sexual relationships before the assault. Your dreams suggest that you're healing, perhaps enough to begin again with... *Is* Brew as hunky as his name?"

Meri had to laugh. "Yes! You sex fiend."

"MOMMY, WHAT'S A BREW?" Trina asked shortly before seven that evening. Meri was changing from baggy jeans and a sweatshirt into a peach-pink sweater and matching wool slacks.

Meri sighed. "I've told you a hundred times today, Trina, so this is the last time. Brew is my student's first name. And *you* should call him Mr. Brodrick."

"I'm too little to say all that," Trina protested. "Brew is easier."

"Please try, sweetheart. Now, after you meet him, you're going to watch television in your room and be quiet while he's here, aren't you?"

Trina twirled a curl of her blond ponytail around one finger. "I know how to make The Disney Channel come on TV."

"Good girl. No switching channels, please."

"What's *his* girl's name, Mommy?"

For the ninety-ninth time that day, Meri answered, "Shannon." She checked herself out in the bedroom mirror, remembering Brew's claim that long legs and small breasts weren't his thing. "As I told you before, Shannon is going to watch the other TV in my study."

"Do I have to call her Mrs. Brodrick?"

"No. She's a teenager, the same age as my students. Put your other bunny slipper on, sweetie."

Meri heard a familiar-sounding engine roar up the driveway and stop outside. She thanked heaven that her grandmother had gone out to dinner with a friend and hoped that on Sunday, Gran would be too busy planning her annual trip to Boston to hear TNT's arrival.

Meri opened the door at the first knock. Brew let Shannon enter first. She wore a T-shirt and tight jeans and looked underwhelmed at spending Friday night in Piedmont with two adults and a child. Meri saw why Brew had said, "One look at her eyes and you know she's mine."

Shannon's were chrome blue, just like her father's, but made up with black eyeliner and rainbow eyeshadow. The same rainbow colors were painted, one shade each, on the girl's long fingernails. Her dark, shoulder-length hair was fluffed and moussed and crimped into masses of miniwaves.

"Hi, Mister Brew. Hi, Shannon," Trina sang out before Meri could say anything. "I'm Katrina Denise Whitworth and I'm very happy to meet you."

Meri gave her a mother's look that said, "Mister Brew" wouldn't do.

"Mister *Brewdrick*, I mean," Trina impishly corrected herself, sticking her hand straight out for Brew to shake.

Meri watched as Brew's big hand swallowed up her daughter's tiny one. His eyes lit up. She'd never seen him genuinely smile before. It affected her as no smile had ever done, much like the first time she'd felt movement in her womb. Her breath caught.

"Yo, Katrina Denise," Brew said, clicking the heels of his black boots together. "I'm buzzed to meet you, too." He gestured at his daughter. "So is Shannon. She's just too cool to show it."

Shannon raised one overpenciled eyebrow and stifled a yawn behind five of her fingernails. "Oh, I'm a real Eskimo, all right." She gave Trina's hand a perfunctory little up-and-down pump and remarked, "I like your rabbit-ear slippers, munchkin."

Trina immediately stepped out of them and offered, "You can wear mine tonight. I have more."

"Yeah?" said Shannon with droll disbelief. "Where's the bunny hutch you hatch them in?"

Trina giggled. "In my bedroom." She reclaimed Shannon's hand and tugged. "I'll show you. I have puppy slippers, too. *And* a Barbie doll."

Like an adolescent Mae West, Shannon rolled her eyes in a blasé arc and wisecracked, "I'd rather see a Ken doll."

Meri noted that Trina's impulsive generosity had warmed Shannon's demeanor. She was almost smiling, and interest sparked in her crystal-clear gaze. Something had clicked between her and Trina. *Bunny slippers and Barbie dolls*, Meri marveled to herself. Who would have guessed?

"Er, this is Meri, Shannon," Brew said. "Emmett's sub."

"I like your manicure, munchkin," Meri deadpanned, hoping that Shannon would find imitation the sincerest form of flattery. It worked.

Shannon grinned sassily. "I'll show you how it's done sometime." Bending, she scooped up the bunny slippers and said to Trina, "Lead me to Ken, small stuff. Or to Barbie if she's all you can scrape up."

Meri watched them troop off to Trina's room. She turned to Brew, who was rubbing the back of his neck.

"She's been so steamed all week I forgot she had teeth to smile with," he muttered. "Talk about mood swings."

"She seems to like three-year-olds more than she thought she would," Meri commented.

Erotic wisps of the dreams she'd had all week flitted through her mind as she looked at the man who had starred in them. She felt short of breath again.

"I like them, too," he responded. "Trina looks like you. Everyone says that, I'll bet."

Meri nodded. "People say the same about you and Shannon, I suppose."

She felt riveted to the floor. Brew looked as dangerous and power packed as he had four nights ago. In fact, everything in the living room seemed smaller with him standing there, and she felt fragile, breakable—and as awkward as a thirteen-year-old.

"Yep," he agreed. "Like father, like daughter. That's me and Shannon." He looked around at Meri's Oriental carpets and ginger-jar lamps, her velveteen sofa, her delicate cherry-wood tables. "Nice place."

He shifted his books from one hand to the other, reminding Meri of her usually perfect Mansfield manners. "Thank you. Would you care for coffee or tea before we start? And may I take your jacket?"

He shrugged out of it, shifting the books again. "Coffee. Black, thanks."

Meri quickly hung his coat in the front closet and motioned him to the sofa. It seemed to shrink to loveseat size the moment he sat down. He didn't look any less imposing in his tight white T-shirt than in his heavy jacket. He leaned forward to put the books on the coffee table, and the flex of his muscular back and shoulders pulled the cotton knit a little tighter. Meri sensed waves of Brew's sexuality enveloping her.

"I'll be back in two minutes," she said, then escaped into the kitchen.

"Need help?" Brew called after her.

"Not at all," she assured him.

She smoothed a hand over her tidy French twist, checking for stray tendrils that might have escaped the pins. Because she knew it was silly to feel untidy and unraveled due to a few inconsequential dreams and one heart-stopping smile, she got busy making coffee, trying to ignore the pounding of her heart.

In the living room, Brew stretched his legs out, crossed his ankles and considered the front of his black jeans. It was looking like stress-management night for the old five-button fly, he mused. Meri looked good enough to eat in that pinky-peachy sweater-and-pants outfit.

She was probably wearing cashmere worth the price of a gold-plated Harley. Probably, the carpet under his boots had cost a few thou, like the tables carved from rare wood. And her underwear was probably hand-made lace from Paris and starched after every wash.

And that hairdo of hers looked like it took some dude an hour and six dozen hairpins to put it together. Sheesh! He reached for his grammar workbook and laid it open over his lap. Damned if he'd advertise that he was hot to see Meri Whitworth's hair tumble down to her shoulders.

She'd never sink to his level, anyway, he reminded himself. Not with the baddest boy in school. Besides, Emmett would be back at the blackboard soon, and then Brew Brodrick would kick back and relax again.

He looked up as Meri came in and set a tray in front of him. He was surprised to see that it wasn't sterling silver. The coffee mugs weren't bone china, either. He squared the book in his lap, and realized the print was upside down. He hoped fervently that she hadn't no-ticed his foul-up, since she was busy taking two soft-drink cans from the tray.

"I'll just run these in to the girls," she said, and disappeared down the hallway.

He had the book righted and his mug balanced on it when she returned a moment later. "Is Shannon be-having herself in there?"

"They're watching a Disney special." She edged into the far corner of the sofa and picked up her coffee mug. "Tell me how you and Emmett handle your sessions together. He called today but couldn't talk long enough to explain."

Brew stared into his cup to stop himself from looking at Meri and sliding closer to her. "We sit at my kitchen table with beer and pretzels and he fills me in on what I missed in class. It goes pretty fast, one-on-one. I don't need to be told anything twice. He's a good guy."

Meri nodded in agreement. "He was my master teacher before I became certified. He's been a close friend since then."

Brew raised an eyebrow and contemplated the rim of his mug. "How close?"

"Nothing romantic. Just good, good friends."

Brew shot a glance at her. "He's no slouch, you're no slouch. What's the hitch? No chemistry?"

"Perhaps." She raised her chin. "Something doesn't mesh, sparks don't strike. Surely that's happened to you."

"Maybe it has." He shrugged as if it hadn't. "Who do you date if you don't date Emmett?"

He was astounding himself, asking so many questions. What did he care who she dated or kissed goodnight or bedded down with after a night on the town?

"I haven't socialized much since my divorce," she replied, her chin lifting a fraction higher.

Brew recognized defenses on the rise when he saw them. That meant she didn't date at all. So what was it with her? Her ex had slapped her around, maybe?

Maybe. It would explain why she always seemed ready to duck a quick fist.

He knew one thing: He wasn't going to aim another question her way. What did he care? *Socialize.* Now there was an upper-crust word for *date*—one meant to put the lower-crust back in its place, for sure.

He leaned forward to set his mug on the coffee table and she jumped at the abrupt movement. "Calm down," he told her, more irritated than he should have been. "What am I? A mugger?"

Two more questions. He snapped his mouth shut.

"I'm . . . sorry," she said. "Caffeine puts me on edge when I least expect it."

"So drink decaf."

"I believe I will from now on." She set her mug down and gestured toward a small alcove to the right. "Shall we move to the dining table and get our lesson under way?"

One look at the narrow table told Brew he'd be rubbing knees with her all night or twisting sideways to avoid contact. The chairs looked like Chippendale or some damn kind no working stiff could ever sit in. Their pricey legs would be gouged by the chain-link trim on his boots.

"Why move?" he questioned. "We're okay here."

Meri didn't feel okay about how easily Brew could slide to her end of the sofa. Then she thought of how the dining alcove would shrink to dollhouse size the moment he sat down. The sofa might be best, after all.

"I'll get my books from the table." She started to rise.

He beat her to her feet. "I'll do it."

White knight at the lady's service again, he taunted himself, unstrung by the chivalrous behavior Meri seemed to bring out in him. First the flat tire, then the free ride home, now moving a stack of schoolbooks. What next for Sir Brew?

Zero, he vowed, unceremoniously dumping the books on the coffee table in front of her and reclaiming his seat.

"Thank you, Brew."

"No sweat," he heard himself say as he fought the urge to slide across the cushions and find out firsthand if Meri's sweater felt as soft over her shoulders and breasts as it looked. He opened his book, wishing Emmett would get the hell out of the hospital before someone did something stupid.

Meri began with the twenty-question pronoun review quiz she'd given the class on Tuesday night. She was surprised when Brew finished it in much less time than the class had. He was looking at her with a knowing eye when she finished scoring the quiz.

"Aced it, didn't I?" he said.

She nodded. "You were obviously paying attention on Monday night." She glanced down at the perfect score she'd marked in red ink at the top of his paper. "How far did you progress before you dropped out of school?"

"How far did Emmett tell you I went?"

"He didn't say. And you haven't answered my question," she added, reminding him that she had a perfect right to inquire about his educational history.

"How's 'Not far' for an answer?" He drummed the eraser end of his yellow pencil on his thigh. "Sometimes I went to school. Most of the time, I didn't."

Meri knew she didn't have any right to ask her next question, but curiosity won out. "What did you do when you didn't?"

"I looked for trouble," he drawled. "And I always found it—every kind you're imagining, and then some." He raised an eyebrow at her. "I stopped short of rape, though, if that's been your big worry about me."

Brew saw her gray eyes widen and noticed how quickly she looked away to place his quiz in a file folder. He recalled his flash of intuition four nights ago and how he'd discounted it as a wrong signal.

"I'm not at all worried, Brew," Meri assured him, forcing herself to speak calmly. "Rape is the last thing on my mind."

"Last on mine, too," he curtly declared. Maybe his street smarts had been wrong, after all. "All I'm thinking about is getting A-plus on my spelling test, so run it past me now and get it over with."

Meri complied with his gruff request and checked his spelling afterward. "Only one wrong," she informed him, pleased that things were going well, at least on the surface. Brew seemed to have accepted her denial.

"One? No way," he protested, sliding sideways to get a look at the test in Meri's hand—and brush his bare arm against the sleeve of her sweater. It was softer than anything he'd ever felt. If cashmere cost a fortune, it was worth every big buck.

Her perfume was making him want to touch his lips to the hollow of her throat. He felt her stiffen and lean away at the touch of his arm and the closeness of his body.

"Where did I screw up?" he murmured, covering her hand with his on the test to angle the paper his way. He felt her tremble. Out of the blue, he wished that she'd lift her lips to the gentle kiss he wanted so badly to place on them.

Gentle because he wanted her to stop shaking and making him feel like a brute she couldn't trust. Gentle because she was supersoft against his arm and smelled like roses. Gentle because she was Emmett's close friend and a little girl's mother and the most frightened, feminine, fragrant female he'd ever been so close to in his rough, tough life.

"What word did I get wrong?" he asked again, firming his hand around hers to hold his test steady enough to make out his spelling error.

Teeth clenched, Meri got out, "Accommodate."

"Ah," he said, his attention on her rather than on the test. "I need two *m*'s instead of one?"

Meri nodded.

"What's so scary about that, I'd like to know?"

She shook her head. "Nothing."

"So *I'm* what's scary, right?"

She managed the barest of nods this time and inched her hand out of his loosening grasp.

"Why, Meri? What makes you so jumpy every time I make a move?"

Pulling in a deep breath, Meri regained enough of her voice to say, "I'm not accustomed to men like you."

"Ex-cuuuse me," he said, his tone hardening. "Dropouts, you mean. Bikers, dumb-ass troublemakers, ex-cons." He slid back to his corner of the sofa. "Well, I'm not *accustomed* to blueblooded babes like you, so we're even on one score."

"That isn't what I meant," Meri said, reaching a tentative hand his way, then drawing back.

It hadn't been entirely terrifying to feel Brew slide so close. Nor had his touch made her want to bolt off the sofa with her heart in her throat. Meri reminded herself that she'd ridden breasts-to-back with him on his bike in safety.

"What I meant was—"

Her halting explanation was cut off by Shannon and Trina traipsing in from the bedroom.

"Whoa," Shannon said to Trina after a single glance at Meri and Brew. "Duck before they start throwing things."

"We need more soda, Mommy," Trina announced, holding two soft-drink cans upside down to prove her point.

Shannon held Trina back by the elbow. "Let's go without seconds, munchkin. The middle of a fight is no place to be, be*lieve* me."

"Two more sodas, coming right up," Meri said, rising none too steadily to her feet.

"I want to get mine," Trina whimpered, her lower lip pushing out. "I can reach."

"Now, Katrina," Meri warned as she saw signs of a temper tantrum on its way. "You can't do it by yourself. You need—"

"*My* help," Shannon cut in. "I'm bigger than you, pipsqueak, so don't give me any lip."

Meri watched, surprised, as Trina's looming tantrum receded and a fit of giggles took its place. She was even more amazed to see Shannon lift Trina into her arms.

Shannon raised her eyebrows at Meri. "Can we help ourselves?"

"*May* we," Brew corrected, at which Shannon just rolled her eyes.

"You may," Meri consented and took her seat again. Given the choice of staying with Brew or inciting one of Trina's infamous outbursts, Brew seemed the wiser choice.

She looked at him after the swing kitchen door had closed behind their daughters. He sat with his arms crossed over his chest.

"Shannon doesn't miss a thing," he mumbled. "Now she knows we don't see eye-to-eye. I'll get needled later about why. She knows the difference between 'can' and 'may,' too. She screws up just to see if I'm on my toes."

"Which you were," Meri said, relieved that the girls had defused the tension. "*She* was certainly better than I was at handling Trina's temper. Trina can throw tantrums that send me right up the wall."

"Yeah. Shannon's mood swings do the same thing to me," Brew acknowledged, uncrossing his arms.

Meri caught the sidelong glance he sent her, then found herself smiling with him, parent to parent.

Brew inclined his head toward the kitchen door. "What's taking them so long in there?"

"The cookie jar, I suspect. I filled it this afternoon with chocolate-chip bars that Santiago baked. They're thinking we've forgotten all about them."

"Who's Santiago?"

"He's Gran's cook."

"He cooks for you, too?"

"No, no. I do my own, except if Trina and I have breakfast with Matilda during the week. She also has a housekeeper and a chauffeur. But Ingrid and Lars don't work for me, if you happen to be wondering."

"What if I am?" Brew countered with a shrug. "You don't look domestic to me."

Meri suddenly wanted to know how she looked to him, but resisted the impulse. She already knew that D cups were his big thing. She began leafing through her teachers' grammar guide.

"Let me see—where did we leave off?"

"Don't you want to know how you look to me, Meri?" Brew almost kicked himself the moment he said it, but Meri's back-to-the-books briskness had irked him after that instant of rapport. He didn't like the way she was ignoring his question, either.

"Well?" he prompted.

"Well, what?" she retorted, annoyed by his persistence. "You made it clear the other night that when you grade bra sizes, A fails and D passes."

"Yeah? So?"

"So, why should I ask how I look to you when I already know?"

"I see where Trina gets her temper," he observed.

"I see where Shannon gets her smart mouth."

"You've missed one thing, Meri."

"And what might that be, Brew?"

"That I stretched the truth the other night."

"You mean D isn't . . . ?" Meri sat back, crossing her arms over her breasts.

"Nope," he confirmed. "D isn't."

No longer indignant, Meri felt suddenly exposed and vulnerable under his measuring blue eyes. "Why did you lie?"

"So you'd quit being a royal pain about me giving you a ride home."

"Why tell the truth now?"

"So you'll remember that I'm an A man, but I didn't do anything about it. Understand?"

She nodded slowly. "I'm sorry I overreacted a while ago."

"Forget it," he said. "Where were we with the grammar?"

But Brew couldn't forget it. When he left with Shannon an hour later, his intuition was whispering "rape" again and he was wishing it would shut up.

Why did Meri have to feel so soft and smell like roses and look like she needed a man who'd make sure she never got hurt again?

5

MERI HAD TROUBLE GETTING to sleep after Brew left Friday night. He was a disturbing man. Finally, she nodded off and had a dream so erotic and explicit that she wakened aroused.

She lay in her bed, feeling the aftereffects of her dream-lover's intimate kisses. Eyes closed, she saw again his black hair fanning across her belly, rippling over her skin with the rhythm of his head. Slowly the dream images faded, along with memory of the pleasuring heat of his mouth.

Meri opened her eyes, stared into the darkness of her bedroom, and closed them again. *Brew.* She folded her arms over the stiff points of her nipples and hugged herself tightly. She pressed her quivering thighs together. *Brew.* Rolling onto her stomach, she rested her flushed face on the cool pillow. *Why can't he stay in his own bed?*

In every dream, he'd whispered, "Anything you want. Anything you need." Each time, she'd wanted and needed more than before. He had never entered her dreams unclothed nor made a move to undress. "I can wait. I can wait," he'd always whispered. Tonight he had taken her further than ever before.

In this dream, it had been easy and natural to respond. In this dream it had been so easy and natural for her to lace her fingers in his hair and accept the gift of his intimate kiss. In real life, she went stiff with fear at a man's touch. What would it take for her to feel normal again?

Not Brew. He was too big, too powerful to control; too massive a force to manage. He also had enough problems of his own. He probably didn't need the complications of a relationship with her.

Meri got out of bed and washed her face. She tied a bathrobe on over her nightgown and padded into her study to try to forget about Brew by working on her thesis. Although it was almost dawn, Trina wouldn't waken till around seven—time enough to write a page or two and index some research footnotes.

The thesis was coming along well enough, although Meri thought it was an uninspired but adequate paper on an uninteresting aspect of secondary education. She had completed nearly a hundred pages of an estimated three hundred. Finished, it would be the length of a short novel.

A novel. She sighed wistfully. In college, she had secretly yearned to major in creative writing, but Gran would never have allowed it. Even teaching high-school English wasn't quite the prestigious public service Gran expected a true-blue Mansfield to render.

Meri turned on her computer and began to read through page ninety-five on the screen. Every word seemed so dry and scholarly.

Her concentration wavered and she thought about Gran's relatives in Boston, who were even more socially correct and straitlaced than Gran. There were Boston Mansfields who were national legislators; one was chief of protocol at the White House. Others were public defense attorneys, dedicated volunteers, executives of charitable foundations. Gran had once told her that marrying Curtis, Sr., and moving from Boston to California with him early in their marriage, had been liberating.

Meri's only memory of Grandad was his funeral, the one time she'd seen Gran cry. She'd been three years old and aware even then that Mansfields kept a stiff upper lip. She'd always wished that her family relationships could be close rather than politely cordial. The sterling Mansfield name was the tie that bound. And there was no escaping the social burdens and high expectations attached to it.

Gran had anticipated greater things from Meri than choosing to teach English. It had been the only major contest of wills she'd ever won against Gran, who'd finally said, "It will do, but barely." Still, as much as she enjoyed teaching, she'd rather write novels.

Novels. To shut out the tempting thought, Meri concentrated again on the dull, lifeless prose she'd written. Only two hundred pages to go. Brew came to mind. She realized she didn't know what his other job was. What did he do besides repair bikes?

It was easier to picture what he'd done last night in her dream than to compile her research notes. As Grace would have advised, Meri let herself think about her dreams. She found herself absently tapping out her thoughts on her keyboard. She stopped and read what she'd just added to page ninety-five of her thesis.

Brew slipped through the door of Meri's bedroom and stood there, drinking in the sight of her with his amazing eyes. The metal studs on his leather jacket reflected the moonlight. They winked tiny silver flashes of light at her as he approached her bed and drew back the sheet. "I've come, Meri," he said in a rich, husky murmur. "Just for you."

Seeing the words on the screen made her dream seem more objective, somehow less personal and disturbing. The heroine did this. The hero did that. He whispered this. She let him do that.

Meri continued to type slowly, but soon her fingers began racing over the keys. She wrote line after line, losing all sense of time and place.

Brew drew his fingers down Meri's throat to the pulse that beat in the hollow there. He circled the tip of his index finger around the indentation and whispered her name. As his touch drifted lower, he whispered other things—evocative suggestions and ravishing promises that made her melt in secret places—made her *want* him. His chrome-blue gaze followed the slow journey of his hand to her bare breast where he—

"Mommy?"

Meri's fingers froze. She jerked out of her trance. A long line of *l*'s formed on the screen after the last word she'd typed. She snatched both hands away from the keyboard and swiveled in her chair.

"Hi, sweetie."

Thumb in her mouth, ragged security blanket clutched against the front of her Care-Bears cartoon pajamas, Trina climbed into Meri's lap and curled up there.

Meri pressed the save-and-exit key on her computer as she cuddled Trina. "Did you have sweet dreams?"

Trina nodded and removed her thumb just long enough to add, "About Shannon. She's funny."

"Yes," Meri agreed. "She has a sense of humor, all right." *A droll, quirky, amusing one.*

"She draws good pictures, Mommy."

"Oh? I didn't know you two drew last night. I thought you just watched Disney and ate every cookie in the jar when I wasn't looking."

Trina giggled as Meri tickled her ribs. "I draw good, too."

"And what did you draw last night, cookie monster?"

"Rain."

"What did Shannon draw?"

"Rain." Trina wriggled out of Meri's arms and tugged at her. "Come see. She wrote pomes, too."

"Poems?" Meri repeated, rising from her chair. Brew's daughter writing poetry? It didn't fit, somehow, with the multicolored manicure and eye shadow. Curious, Meri followed Trina down the hall and into her bedroom.

Down on all fours, Trina reached under the pink dust-ruffle on her canopy bed and pulled out several drawings done in bright marker colors. "See?" said Trina, spreading them out on the pink-elephant bedspread. "Rain."

Meri immediately saw whose rain was whose. Trina's was a flurry of fat, blue blobs with an orange sun shining behind them. Shannon's were teardrop-shaped and exquisitely iridescent, each drop distinct from the other, each animated by a little smile. All fell at the same slant from a pearlescent cloud.

What caught Meri's eye and held it, though, was the four-line poem Shannon had written in one large raindrop at the very center of the charmed storm.

I laugh with raindrops,
Drunk with the fun of them,
And hold in my two hands
Onehundredand one ofthem

Meri stood there transfixed. Had Shannon read this somewhere before? She was willing to bet it was original.

"Shannon made a hundred and *one* rains," Trina said. "We counted. What do the words say, Mommy?"

Reading them aloud, Meri felt even more strongly their simple power and the emotions they evoked. Joy in nature's beauty. The one drop apart from the many, yet a part of the many, as well. Though she worked with gifted girls at the Pacific School, Meri had seldom seen a poem like this cross her desk. She had never seen one by a D student.

"We'll have to save these in a special place," Meri told Trina. The poem was too precious to lose. She gathered up the drawings, resolved to somehow find out more from Shannon on Sunday night about the poem.

If it was her own creation, Shannon should be getting *A*'s in English, if in no other subject.

A knock at the front door sent Trina racing out, declaring, "I'll get it."

Meri caught up with her in the living room and pulled her up short. "*I* answer the door, remember? Never, never open it yourself, Trina. Never."

Trina's lip pushed out, her heels dug into the carpet. The knock sounded again, followed by Matilda calling, "Yoo-hoo. Rise and shine."

"Coming," Meri called back.

Trina sucked her lip in halfway. "It's Great-Gran. Can I open the door now?"

"Yes, you may, but only because it's Great-Gran."

"Rise'n'shine, Great-Gran," Trina greeted, flinging the door wide open.

"Bare feet on a chilly morning, Katrina?" Matilda inquired as she entered. "Run put your slippers on, child, and a robe, too."

Trina skipped away.

"Katrina needs far more discipline, Merideth. She'll have another cold before you know it. But that's not why I popped in. I have only a moment before I'm off for the day."

Meri was glad of that. Matilda's lectures, though well-intentioned and conscientious, could be lengthy. Gran was wearing a crimson Chanel suit. Meri asked, "Off to what for the day?"

"A Red Cross benefit breakfast, to begin with," Matilda replied. "Then a symphony luncheon and too much more to list right now. I'm knocking to see if you thought to invite Emmett's special student to Sunday tea. My guests will be the Fairchilds from Hillsborough, more open-minded than most. If you've invited the man—"

"I haven't, Gran. He's very busy with two jobs and a teenage daughter and Emmett's classes." Meri spread her hands. "So much to do and so little time, poor man. It seemed unfair to put him on the spot for tea."

"Well, I do dislike last-minute guests, as you know. How did his lessons proceed last evening?"

"Very well."

"And when will you meet next with him?"

"Sunday evening."

Meri decided right then that the carriage house would be the wrong setting for Brew's future lessons. She could just hear the lecture she'd receive concerning TNT and Shannon's makeup and manicure—not to mention Brew, himself—if Matilda happened to "pop in" while they were present. It wasn't her habit in the evenings, but trusting past history might be tempting fate.

As soon as Matilda had left, Meri picked up the phone and dialed the number Emmett had given her. Brew answered on the first ring.

"Yeah?"

After writing about him this morning, Meri was taken aback at actually hearing his voice. It held no hint of the dream-lover whispers she'd heard in her sleep. It was gruff, gravelly and impatient.

"Um, Brew, this is Meri Whitworth. The reason I'm calling is—"

"I already know why," he cut in. "I left my jacket there last night and you don't want it crowding up your closet."

Meri blinked. He'd left it?

"I'll stop by on my way to work and get it," he said. "Thirty minutes, max." He hung up.

Meri stared at the receiver in her hand, then dropped it into its cradle. She hadn't noticed that he'd walked out last night without his jacket.

He must have realized he was without it the moment he mounted the bike. Why hadn't he come back for it before he drove off?

She opened the closet. There it was. Black leather with a broken zipper. She touched the metal-stud pattern on the upper sleeve, reminded of them reflecting silver moonlight in her dreams. Quickly she shut the door. *Thirty minutes, max.* He'd be roaring into the driveway soon.

"Trina," she called. "Get dressed, sweetie. Mr. Brodrick forgot something last night. He's coming to get it."

"SO THAT'S WHY YOU FROZE your buns off all the way home last night," Shannon observed when Brew hung up. "A perfecto excuse to see Meri again before Sunday."

"Can it, Shannon," he snapped. "I didn't call Meri. She called me. I'd have done without until Sunday and you know it."

She retorted saucily, "I know she's beautiful and nice and you think so, too. Say hi to Trina for me."

"I'll do that," Brew replied before heading for a quick shower. "And you behave yourself. I'm going to call you here every few minutes after I get to work. If you don't pick up the phone every time . . ."

Shannon grimaced. "I'll *answer*, okay?"

He made sure Shannon got a good look at his dark morning shadow and the ragged elbow-holes in his black sweater before he left her pouting over her morning coffee. He wasn't going to encourage her idea that he couldn't wait to see Meri. She was always this way after he'd grounded her, but her attitude still peeved him.

Warm in his thick sweater, he mounted TNT and sped out of Berkeley, into Oakland and up into the Piedmont hills to Matilda's estate. He didn't need his black leather to get through the weekend. So what? If Meri hadn't called, he'd be on his way to work.

He pulled up to her house and hung his helmet on the bike. *So . . . will her hair be up or down this morning?*

Down. It was sleek and blond and hung past her shoulders. She wore no cashmere today—gray denim jeans and a lighter-gray blouse that matched her eyes. She looked so damned good—and even a little happy to see him.

He rubbed the stubble on his jaw, wishing he'd shaved. "Hi, Meri."

"Come in, Brew."

He stepped over the doorsill, shoving his sweater sleeves up to the elbows to hide the holes. "Nice day," he said.

She nodded. "So nice that it's too bad you have to work."

"Yeah," he agreed. "If I didn't, I could go out and play like you probably get to do."

"Oh, no playing for me," Meri corrected. "Just writing." Realizing she wasn't making much sense, she added, "Writing my thesis for my master's degree, I mean."

Brew stood looking at her, wanting to take her out on TNT for the day. Her long hair would blow free in the sun and wind behind them. He'd feel her arms around him, her small breasts warming his back—and more—again. He'd better get out of here.

"Where's Trina?" he asked, looking around to keep his eyes off Meri. "Shannon gave me a message for her."

"She's in the kitchen, making hot chocolate just for you. I told her you wouldn't have time, but she insisted, and . . . I hoped you might . . . Would you have just a sip before you go?"

"I'm crazy for hot chocolate," Brew lied. "I've got loads of time." That last part was the truth. He called his own hours at work. Meri's smile made him think about skipping work all day. He'd leave right after the cocoa.

Meri led him to the kitchen where Trina was kneeling on a chair, busily arranging a child-size plastic teapot and little matching cups on the table. "Hi, Mr. Brewdrick."

"Call me Brew," he said. "Everyone does."

"Brew," she repeated. "I told Mommy Brew is easy. My mouth is too little for big names."

Brew laughed. Trina giggled, pleased with her wit. Meri laughed along with them. This was the first time she'd seen Brew laugh.

"What are you brewing up there?" He bent over to sniff at the pot. "Beer?"

"No." Trina wrinkled her nose. "Chocolate. Sit down." She darted a glance at Meri, and added, "Please."

He did, and Meri sat opposite him. Under the table her knees bumped into his. She swung her eyes away; so did Brew.

She fixed her attention on the little teapot. She held her breath as Trina tilted the pot to the first cup, hoping she wouldn't spill. It was hard to breathe, anyway, after that brush of knees.

Trina poured shakily into all three cups and set the pot down with a thump. "One for you," she said, wobbling a cup over to Brew. "And one for you." She delivered another just as precariously to Meri. "And one for me."

Brew pinched the tiny handle between his big thumb and forefinger and raised his cup. "Cheers."

Meri and Trina echoed him and they all sipped.

"Never had it so good," Brew said, licking his lips. "Thank you, Katrina Denise."

"I cooked it special for you," Trina said, preening at his praise.

"I know." Brew looked over the table at Meri and nudged her knee with his. "Your mommy told me."

Meri almost dropped her cup. He saw pink tinge her aristocratic cheekbones and the smooth column of her throat. She looked flustered as she slid her chair back and rose.

"Brew has work to do, Trina," she said. "We mustn't keep him." He had the longest legs in the world, she was thinking, and right now her kitchen was the smallest room on earth. "Have a second cup of chocolate while I see him to the door. Say goodbye."

"Bye, Brew."

He stood and looked down at Trina. "Before I split, Shannon says hi."

"Say hi back." Trina began stacking the cups and saucers. "I like Shannon. She's cool."

Meri said, "A brand-new word from last night. At this age, words go in one ear and come right out the mouth."

"I hope it's the only four-letter one she learned."

"I know the F-word," Trina announced. "Lars says it to Santiago in Great-Gran's kitchen."

"The less said at the moment, the better," Meri advised as Brew came around the table. "I'll get your jacket."

"Sorry it smelled up your closet all night," he said, watching the sway of Meri's slim hips as he followed her out of the kitchen.

"It did no such thing," Meri objected.

"Why did you phone me to come and get it, then?"

"I didn't phone you about this," she replied, removing the jacket from its hanger. "I called to say I think it's best if we meet at your place on Sunday night."

"Oh." He stood there feeling like a geek. "Why didn't you say so on the phone?"

"You hung up before I could." She held the jacket out to him. "Is a change of scene all right with you?"

"A change?" He looked around the room, then took the jacket from her. "Whatever's fair."

"Emmett gave me your address," she said. "I'll be there at seven. Before I forget, thank you for indulging Trina's chocolate whim."

"No sweat off my back," he said with a shrug.

"I should also apologize, Brew. I forgot I'd put your jacket away last night. You shouldn't have been so polite by not reminding me when you left."

"It wasn't a manners thing," he said after a pause. "It was a cool excuse to drop in for cocoa."

Her brilliant smile was his reward for daring to reveal two-thirds of the truth. So he'd wanted an excuse to drop in. Big deal. She was beautiful, and had a cute kid. She was nothing he'd ever had and everything he'd started to want since Monday night.

It wasn't his fault; it was Emmett's fault for asking her to sub.

At this rate, Sunday night would be a long time coming.

6

"THIS PLACE IS A DUMP," Brew declared on Sunday afternoon. The apartment walls needed a new coat of paint, the floors were unwaxed, the couch and chairs needed slipcovers to conceal worn spots.

Shannon was lying on the couch reading a magazine. She replied, "It is not. The dishes are washed, the sheets are clean, everything's dusted. Sure, it's not Piedmont, but—"

"Who's comparing?" Brew cut in.

"You, Brew. You made Joe clean up the shop downstairs and now you're looking at *me* like I'm supposed to sew new curtains or something because Meri's coming tonight."

Brew rubbed the back of his neck. "Her place is damn nice, Shannon."

"So is Meri. Not like the snob I expected." Her tone softened. "She won't compare when she gets here, I'll bet. We could get some posters, maybe, before tonight. Fresh flowers, stuff like that." She slid him a shrewd glance. "I could use a new Mariah Carey CD. Feel like a Sunday shopping spree?"

He shrugged. "You feel like one?"

"Only if a CD is part of the deal. We've never fixed this place up before. Why now?"

"Why not?" he countered. "It needs it, that's for sure."

"Brew, try not answering questions with questions. You're my father. If you have a thing for Meri, I have a right to know."

"Hey, if I want to redecorate, I'll redecorate."

Shannon sat up and tossed her magazine aside. "I get the message. I'm going to wear my Born To Shop shirt. You put the saddlebags on TNT."

"They're already on," said Brew. "Let's go."

MERI PARKED THE JUG in front of the bike shop at seven that evening and gathered up her books. The windows of The Last Detail were dark, but light glowed from the windows of the apartment above. Directly across the street from The Last Detail was an automotive-parts warehouse. A deli adjoined it on the corner, its neon sign advertising soup, sandwiches and *gelato* to go. Like the bike shop, the deli and warehouse were closed.

Meri got out of the Jug and locked it. She heard a dog bark as she approached the shop door. Brew hadn't mentioned a guard dog.

The door opened before she rang the bell. In the dark doorway she saw a white smile, a white T-shirt. Brew. Startled by his sudden appearance, she stepped back. As she did, the top book on her pile slid off and hit the sidewalk with a sharp slap.

"Oh!" she gasped.

"Woof! Woof!" barked the dog.

"Cool it, Scrounge," Brew said, reaching out to steady Meri.

She regained her balance, then dropped to her knees to retrieve the fallen book. Brew did the same at the same instant. Her forehead bonked his. Another book toppled from the stack.

"Hold it, hold it," he ordered, his hands gripping her shoulders to steady her again. "Stay still."

He lifted Meri slowly to her feet. Her hair was down and she wore the same sweater as before, but with a print skirt this time. When he smelled her rose perfume, he thought about pulling her close and saying he was sorry he'd been too impatient to wait for the bell to ring.

"I'm so sorry," she stammered, one hand at her throat. "The door opened so fast that I—"

"I should've turned on a light so you could see me," he cut in. "*I'm* sorry, okay?"

"Woof!"

"That's Scrounge. She's harmless. You just stand in one spot and I'll get the books."

Brew let go of her gingerly, as if afraid she might topple, then bent to scoop up the books. He wished then that Meri had worn pants instead of a skirt. His close-up view of her ankles and calves shadowed by light from above made him want to skim his palms up their sleek curves from the low heels of her pumps to the soft warmth of her inner thighs.

Breathing hard, he lifted her books and tucked them under his arm. "How's your head?"

"No damage done," she said, touching her forehead. "And yours?"

"No dents. Come on in." He braced the door open with one knee and reached in to flip a light switch.

Overhead fluorescents came on and Meri saw motorcycles of every size and color in various states of repair clustered around four work stations. She smelled grease and paint and a faint odor of gasoline in the long room.

"We do a lot of customizing here," Brew said after he reset the security alarm. "And some restoring," he added. "Antique bikes are my job whenever they come in. I'm putting three back in shape next week for a collector. All Harleys."

Meri had never thought of motorcycles as antiques or collector's items. Aware of how little she knew of Brew's world, she followed him through the shop to the narrow stairway at the rear. Near the foot of the stairs, on a big beanbag pillow, a dog sat up and wagged its tail. Its swollen nipples and a very round abdomen showed it was a female.

"Meet the junkyard dog," Brew said. "Scrounge, shake hands."

Scrounge held her shaggy paw out and Meri shook it, smiling. "When is she due?"

"Any day now."

"How did she get pregnant?"

Brew raised an eyebrow. "How do you think?"

"I meant—" Meri flushed "—why isn't she spayed instead of pregnant?"

"Because Joe's Catholic and doesn't believe in birth control for dogs or people. He owns the shop. She's his dog."

"I see. Has Joe arranged for the puppies to go to good homes?"

"Yep. He's got more orders than Scrounge may be able to fill this time."

"Well, that's good to know," Meri said, smiling as Scrounge licked her hand. "She looks the way I felt after nine months of carrying Trina."

Brew pictured Meri pregnant. He wondered what she was like in bed. It wasn't the first time he'd wondered *that*.

"After you." He gestured for her to go up the stairs. "Watch your step. They're steep."

"This is quite convenient, living above your workplace," she commented.

"Can't beat a short commute," he agreed, watching her slender ankles precede him, imagining how they'd feel, one locked over the other against the small of his back. This thing he had for Meri Whitworth was bed news. *Bad* news, he corrected. He couldn't even think straight anymore.

He stretched past Meri at the landing to open the apartment door. She reached for the doorknob an instant before he did and his hand landed over hers. He slowly turned both the knob and her hand until the latch clicked. He felt her go very still.

"Brew . . ."

"What?" He kept his hand on hers. Her books in his other hand were heavy. He wanted to drop them and slide that hand along her ribs and under her breasts. One step forward would bring his chest flush against her back. He took a deep breath. He didn't drop the books or take that step.

"Brew, don't—" she took a deep breath "—crowd me."

"I'm only touching your hand, Meri." He stroked his fingertips over her rigid knuckles. "What's the problem? Me?"

She bowed her head. "No."

"Your ex? He took his fists to you or something?"

"No." She rested her forehead against the door. "It's *my* problem. It's personal. Let's go in. Please."

"Before we do, tell me how I'm supposed to stay five feet away from you at all times. You're so nerved up it makes me nerved up. What am I supposed to do?"

The feel of her skin, the scent of her perfume—he was beginning to think he couldn't stay an inch away from her if his life depended on it. He was asking for answers he shouldn't want. Caring more than he should care. He had a thing for this woman and it was getting hard to handle.

"I'm doing my best, Brew."

"But you're still feeling cornered," he said. He moved back and withdrew his hand with gruff impatience. "So give the door a push and let yourself in. Don't let me stop you."

Meri pushed but the door didn't give. She pushed harder, then harder still, without success. "It must be locked."

"It must be you need my help," he retorted, pushing on the door.

The stubborn door gave way and opened into a small kitchen. Meri had a quick impression of blue checkered curtains and a matching tablecloth before Brew guided her through saloon-style swing doors to his living room. There she saw a couch and chairs with glenplaid slipcovers, a cheerful rag rug on the polished wood floor, a bouquet of daisies on the console TV, another of pink roses on a lamp table.

"Why, this is charming," she said. "What lovely roses."

Brew followed Meri's sincere gaze of approval from the roses to the scenic posters on the walls. He silently blessed Shannon. She knew what went with what, that kid. But the roses had been strictly his idea. He still had thorns in his thumbs from fitting two dozen stems into that new glass vase.

The place didn't look super-duper, of course, he observed with a critical eye. But it looked better than before. He decided to paint every wall before Meri came the next time. If she'd be coming back.

"May I smell the roses? They're my favorite of all flowers."

"Help yourself."

He tried not to watch as she stepped over and touched her nose to her favorite flowers. He should put her books down on the new slipcover of the couch. He didn't. She turned and caught him staring.

Turning away to hide the blush his stare had provoked, Meri inhaled more of the scent and murmured, "Rose is the most wonderful fragrance."

Didn't he know? Didn't he wish he didn't know? Her cheeks were the same pink as those petals. Her sweater and skirt were close to the same color. And her hair looked like pure sunshine and moonbeams under the table lamp. He decided the kitchen would be a good place to be right now—alone.

"Something to drink? Wine, beer?" He managed to wink. "Hot chocolate?"

Meri straightened. "A beer would be a nice change. That's what you have when Emmett comes, right?"

"Right." He was surprised that she'd remembered. "And pretzels. You like big soft ones with mustard?"

"I'm sure I will." Meri sat on the couch next to the books Brew had placed there. Opening one, she pretended to scan the table of contents while he retreated to the kitchen.

Then she looked around the room a second time. The slipcovers and rug looked as new and untouched as the curtains and tablecloth in the kitchen. The daisies and roses appeared to be first-day fresh. Underlying their fragrance was the unmistakable lemon scent of floor wax and furniture polish.

Brew had gone to considerable effort for her visit. She wished that he hadn't taken such pains, yet felt flattered that he had. How sweet of him. *Sweet.* Funny, she'd never thought of him in that way.

Nor had she thought of him as self-conscious enough to spit and polish. Were the roses his way of saying he'd noticed her rose perfume and liked it? If so, how romantic of him. Only in her dreams had he been romantic. Those dreams . . .

She hadn't been able to stop writing about them since Saturday morning. Yesterday and all day today, she had added to the first page she'd written. It had all begun to take the form of a novel. In her mind, it was titled *Dark Brew.* Part dream, part reality, it had become a chronicle of her experience of Brew from the moment she had locked gazes with him on Monday night.

One week. Had it been only seven days since that first moment? In retrospect, it seemed longer—and shorter—and confusing. So many buried feelings and emotions had surfaced in response to him. So many painful memories. Such erotic dreams. So much to sort out and write out that she'd temporarily abandoned her thesis. *Back on track tomorrow,* she told herself.

She caught her breath slightly as Brew shouldered through the swing doors with beer and pretzels on a tray. His jeans looked almost new, pale blue. They were the low-riding, button-fly style that drew female eyes if a man filled them out in the right places. Like Brew did . . . Meri quickly looked away.

Brew sat down and placed two tall glasses and a plate of bagel-size pretzels on the low table in front of her. The beer in each glass was dark brown with a creamy head of foam. The pretzels had drizzles of yellow mustard on their rock-salted tops.

Brew picked up his glass. He tipped the lip of it to Meri's. "Cheers."

Meri returned the toast. "You're sure this isn't root beer?"

"Taste it. You'll see it's not kid stuff."

Meri tasted, then raised her eyebrows in surprise. "Mmm. Delicious. So different from commercial brands."

"Thanks. I made it."

Though Meri had heard of home brew, she had never quite imagined anyone bothering. "You did? Really?"

"Really," he confirmed. "That's what I do five days a week, sometimes six. I work downstairs for Joe four nights a week."

"You mean making beer is your day job?"

"Yah, I'm head brewer for three brew-pubs. They're lower-rent versions of upscale microbrewers. Ever heard of the Gordon Biersch brewery restaurants?"

Meri nodded. "I've been to Gordon Biersch in Palo Alto. The brewing tanks were right there."

"Have a good time?"

"Wonderful. It was St. Patrick's Day, as I recall. Very festive. Great menu."

"Good guys, Gordon and Biersch," he said. "You'd like Brews, too."

"Brews? The pubs have your name?"

"Naw. That's just coincidence. There are Brews in San Francisco, Palo Alto and San Jose. More locations are in the works. Keeps me hopping."

She laughed at his pun. "You must have a million one-liners like that."

"I've kegged a few," he conceded, laughing with her.

"Now I know what Emmett meant when he said you're a real beer expert. I imagined chugalug contests at biker conventions, I'm afraid—nothing like what you've just told me. It must be fascinating work."

He nodded. "I like it."

"How did you get interested in brewing beer?"

"Prison. My buzz name was already Brew by then. You were right about the chugalugs and biker bashes, but that was before I wised up. Anyway, in two years behind bars, I read a lot. I missed my beer, so I read everything I could get my hands on about it. I came out with an education, got a grunt job with a brewery and worked my way up."

"How long have you been head brewer for Brews?"

"Six years. I've moonlighted downstairs pretty steady for eight. Joe took the first chance on me when I got out of prison. Charged me cheap rent for this place. He's a lot like Emmett. The heart-of-gold type."

"Is head brewer as high as you can go?"

"No. One step above is master brewer. It's a licensed position in Europe but not in the U.S. I'll make it someday. I'll be part-owner of a pub, too, if I stick with it." Brew held the plate out to her. "You're not eating your pretzel."

Meri took one and felt his gaze swerve across the front of her sweater before he put the plate down and helped himself. She bit into the soft, chewy pretzel, thinking of how Brew had bared her breasts in her dreams. She had felt the smooth surface of his leather jacket against her nipples, the graze of the broken zipper each time he lowered his mouth to her body.

"Delicious," she murmured. It was wiser to think of something other than her dreams, so she counted back. Brew was thirty-two now, so he was twenty-four when he'd left prison and started working for Joe.

Meri's first bite of pretzel had left a dot of mustard behind on her upper lip. Brew debated whether to reach a fingertip out to it, or to kiss it. *Ignore it,* he told himself. He couldn't. His fingertip itched. He pulled in a deep breath.

Just hand her a damn napkin, he told himself, then realized he'd forgotten to bring any from the kitchen. Thinking clearly hadn't been easy in there. It was no simpler now. She'd spook if he reached out.

He wondered whether her "personal" problem was a fist-happy ex-husband . . . or rape. He thought of any man doing either to Shannon or Meri, and couldn't swallow. He realized then that Meri wasn't the only one with a problem. He had one, too. He wanted her to trust him, to laugh with him and have a good time. The only other time he'd felt this bighearted was the day Shannon had turned up on his doorstep. He was in trouble. Deep trouble.

"You've got mustard right here," he said, pointing to the corresponding spot on his own lip.

She touched a finger to her lip and wiped it away. "Thank you."

"No sweat. I hate it when that happens and people say zilch about it. You don't know until you get home."

"I hate that, too." She smiled and pointed to the left corner of her mouth. "You have some right here."

Brew deliberately wiped the opposite corner of his mouth. He then picked up his beer so that both hands would be occupied. "Gone?"

"No. Wrong side."

"Help me out, would you?" He jutted his chin in her direction and tried to look helpless. He prompted, "I'm like Scrounge. I won't bite."

Tentatively, Meri opened her hand. Reaching out would be a step toward normalcy. She knew that she'd have wiped the mustard away for him before the rape. There was no valid reason to balk now. *Reach.* She lifted her hand to the corner of Brew's mouth. He moved forward to meet her touch.

"Gone," she said, holding her finger in midair after an instant of contact. Before the rape, would she have touched her tongue to the bit of mustard? Only if the man in question had already captured her interest.

Only if she'd wanted him to know it. What would Brew make of it if she did?

Before she could decide, he brushed her hovering fingertip with his pretzel, saying, "Back where it belongs."

Meri sat back, short of breath. She took a long drink of her beer. So much for returning to any normal behavior with a man. She'd almost taken a practical step in that direction but had dithered and debated instead. Maybe she'd never be normal again, except in her dreams.

"So, tell me what I missed last class," Brew said, because thinking about sliding closer to Meri was too much on his mind.

Meri described the exercises the class had gone through. "Which would you like to work on first?" she asked.

"The reading comprehension."

Meri gave him a short essay to read, then asked questions about content and meaning. After he answered each question easily and correctly, she looked up at him, puzzled.

"The rest of the class had much more difficulty with this, Brew. With your spelling and reading skills at a high level, why are you in this class at all? How did you fail the pretest for this section of the GED?"

He shrugged. "Beats me. Maybe school's doing me some good. Who knows?"

Meri frowned. His reply to her query was too flip to explain his performance. His comprehension answers were articulate and intelligent. His two spelling tests so far had been almost perfect. What was going on here?

She proceeded with punctuation, then a written composition, and ended with spelling, as before. Brew did an excellent job on everything.

"At this rate, you should have passed the pretest when you took it," she said.

"Well, I didn't, Meri. I blew the language-arts pretest along with social studies, science and math." He directed a raised eyebrow at her. "Ask Shannon. She went with me when I tested."

Shannon. Meri had forgotten all about the girl. "Where *is* Shannon?"

"In her room doing homework. I told her not to show her face until it's done and I see it. At her speed, that'll be tomorrow just before school."

"Is she truly a *D* student?"

He nodded. "It's an improvement, considering she was an *F* student when she lived with her mother. I keep thinking the only way for her is up. That's not how she thinks, though."

"Is she unhappy here with you?"

Brew shook his head. "Happy as a clam compared to how she was with her mother and stepfather. He had a quick fist."

Meri thought of Shannon's poem—the contrast between its excellence and her poor grades. Shannon's mother had been Brew's foster mother. "Do you mind telling me why Shannon came to live with you?"

Brew looked away, considering how to word his reply. Meri had no experience with juvenile delinquency, foster homes, or the juvenile justice system. She had no idea what could happen to a kid whose skid-row parents had overdosed together on heroin before he was seven years old.

What was there to tell about Shannon, her mother, and himself but the cold, bitter facts? It wasn't a pretty story. But if Meri couldn't take a big dose of real life, that would be *her* problem. Wouldn't it?

"Her mother—my foster mother—seduced me by accident," Brew said. "I was a stupid kid, big for my age and full of it. I liked her more than any of the six foster mothers I'd had before her. I hated my foster father because he beat her up when he got drunk.

"Anyway, I comforted her one day and wound up in bed with her. Tessa was forty, almost forty-one. I was sixteen, almost seventeen." He took a long swallow of beer and looked over at Meri. "Shocked? Wishing you'd never asked?"

Quietly she said, "I'm wishing things could have been different for you and Tessa."

"If they'd been different, I wouldn't have Shannon now. It's no piece of cake, but I'm glad to be her father."

"You didn't know she existed until a year ago?"

"You're full of questions tonight, Meri."

She pressed one hand to her mouth in immediate self-reproach. "I'm sorry. I shouldn't have probed into your private life."

"Hey, I didn't mean you should feel bad about it. I answered what you asked, didn't I? You weren't twisting my arm."

She began collecting his work sheets. "You should have cut me off at the first rude question."

"Maybe I didn't think it was rude. Hell, if anyone's been rude, I'm it. No napkins, no offer of another beer for the last hour, no—"

"You've been a perfect gentleman, Brew. One beer is enough. I'm driving home tonight. As for napkins, pretzels hardly require formality."

"Me? A perfect gentleman? There's one I've never heard."

Meri stacked her books. "Your behavior has been sterling. The same can be said of your taste in roses. My prying, on the other hand, was nothing of the sort. Certainly not worthy of a Mansfield."

"We can even the score real quick if I ask what *your* problem is. Feel like giving a perfect gentleman an answer to that rude question, Meri?"

Meri's movements slowed. She carefully placed the last book on top of the rest. "That's no more your business than your relationship with your foster mother is mine."

"Would it explain why I get the feeling that someone—a man—was violent with you? You react a lot like Tessa used to at a sudden move."

"I never discuss my ex-husband, Brew," Meri said, to mislead him.

"Which makes *me* a big loose-lips for discussing my teenage sex life," he retorted.

Feeling utterly miserable at the inadvertent embarrassment she had caused Brew, Meri rose from the couch with her books in hand.

"I really must go, Brew. Thank you for the beer and pretzels. I'll see you in class tomorrow night."

"Don't count on it," he said, his expression dark and insolent as he came to his feet. "I have better things to do than watch you ride your high horse."

"I didn't mean to sound superior."

"Sure, you didn't." He held a hand out for her books. "Give me those. The last thing I want is a klutz dropping them down the stairs on the way out."

Knowing she deserved that put-down, Meri handed the books to him. She stood aside as he yanked the kitchen door open and flipped a light switch, then preceded him down the stairs.

Down below, Scrounge tried to sit up, then flopped back on the big beanbag, panting. Meri noticed the dog's rolling eyes and lolling tongue, then saw a small, dark shape squeeze out from under Scrounge's quivering tail.

"Brew!" Meri stopped abruptly.

"Watch it, dammit," he said. Books went thudding end over end down the stairs as he clutched at the railing to keep his footing. "For God's sake, Meri! Can't you—?"

"Puppies, Brew! They're coming. It's time."

Brew peered down over Meri's shoulder at Scrounge. "Oh, hell. You're right."

Meri turned to look up at him. "What do we do?"

"I don't know. Don't *you?* You're a woman. You've had a baby."

"I've never had puppies," Meri teased, tiptoeing down the stairs. Scrounge was inspecting and licking the first new arrival clean. "How many puppies did Scrounge have the last time?"

"Six. I was at work. By the time I saw them they were all born and living it up."

"Brew, look." Meri knelt at the beanbag. "Here comes the second one."

"I'll pass," Brew said, sitting down a few steps up from the bottom. "I've never seen anything get born."

Meri knelt there, marveling. "It's a miracle you shouldn't miss. Really, Brew." She stretched one hand toward him. "Come down. Trust me, it's truly something to see. Scrounge seems to know what to do."

"Yeah? That's good." Brew waved Meri's outstretched hand away. He looked a bit woozy. "I'll sit this one out."

Surprised, Meri looked up at him. Men—even the strongest and most masculine, it seemed—could be floored by the sight of a female giving birth.

"Come down, you big coward," she coaxed. "If Scrounge can stand the pain, surely you can stand one look at the mystery and miracle of life."

Meri stifled a chuckle when she saw Brew's expression change as he pulled together the shreds of his male ego.

"No woman calls me coward," he growled, buttbumping down the stairs to take a look at the purported miracle. "No man does, either. No one, Meri. You hear me?"

Meri nodded. "I hear you. Here comes number three."

"My sweet Lord," Brew said after a wary moment watching Scrounge's performance. A stunned silence followed before he said, "Look at that. Brand spanking new."

Meri was never sure quite how it happened, but by the time pup number four emerged into the world, Brew's arm was curled around her shoulders. The first three pups were beginning to nurse.

She giggled when Brew observed, "Scrounge is popping them out like sausages."

"I didn't bring Trina into the world that easily," she assured him. "Fourteen hours of labor. Nothing can describe the pain or the joy of the first moment I held her."

Brew sighed. "I wish I'd been there when Shannon was born. I wish I'd seen her grow up. My first moment was when I opened the door last year. There was this gorgeous kid with my eyes and hair looking at me. I thought I was seeing things. She stood right at the top of these stairs and said, 'Tessa is my mom. I think you're my dad.'" Scrounge was lying down again. "Here comes number five. Look."

"Yes. I see." Meri was acutely aware of Brew's arm circling tighter around her shoulders, of his eyes turning from the newest arrival to look at her.

"Your perfume smells as good as you look," he murmured.

Feeling his warm breath stir the hair at her ear as he spoke, she remembered the hot, harsh whispers she heard almost four years ago. She panicked and abruptly got up out of Brew's embrace.

"It's late. I have to go."

"Have to—?" Brew missed having her tucked into the curve of his arm. "Why?" he inquired, looking at her. "Because I think you smell and look good?"

"Yes." She edged away, clutching her shoulder bag to her side. "I must go before . . ."

Brew came to his feet. "Before what, Meri?"

"Before it gets later. Gran will worry. She'll call. Trina will—" She stopped rambling to swallow back the inordinate swell of panic and fear in her throat. "My books, please, Brew."

"Can't you wait for Scrounge to finish making miracles?"

"No, I can't now. I shouldn't have lingered in the first place. I shouldn't have let you—"

She broke off in confusion. Brew looked up from gathering her books. "Do what? Get close enough to touch?" He straightened and handed her the pile of books. "What did the bastard you married do to you?"

"Nothing I ever discuss." She turned and rushed through the shop to the door.

"Hold it!" Brew caught her elbow before she touched the doorknob. "The burglar alarm's on. You want every cop in Berkeley here in three minutes?"

"No, of course not."

"Give me a sec to turn it off, then. But before I do, tell me one thing."

A few more seconds and Meri knew her voice would shake. A minute more and she'd be stretching the limits of her hard-won control. "All I want to do is go, Brew."

"I see that. *I* want to know why. One minute we're cozy, the next minute we're not. You have a boyfriend you forgot to mention?"

She shook her head.

After a still, silent moment, he asked, "You have a girlfriend, maybe?" She shook her head again. He deactivated the alarm.

Meri said a faint "good night" and hurried out to the Jug. She drove away as soon as it warmed up. Without looking back she knew Brew was standing at the door, watching until her taillights disappeared. He'd probably go back upstairs and dump the roses he'd bought just for her.

If he showed up for class tomorrow night, he'd be a ticking time-bomb.

7

CLASS STARTED ON MONDAY night without Brew in attendance. He didn't arrive until after the five-minute break, when everyone was back in their seats and silently reading a short story.

When the door slowly opened, Meri knew without looking up whose hand was on the doorknob. She knew who wore the boots when she heard the soft, metallic clink of chain trim as they headed to the last desk in the back row. She knew who dropped the motorcycle helmet to the floor after he sat down.

She refused to meet the chrome-blue eyes she knew were lazily, insolently checking her out.

It was Charleston who looked up and said to the latecomer, "What's happening, my man?"

"Same old, same old," the deep rumble of Brew's voice replied. "What's with you?"

"Hey, guys," Arlene mildly interjected. "*Some* people here are trying to read, okay?"

Meri looked up then and spoke to Charleston and Arlene. "Children," she said in her sweetest, most bantering tone. "Do be nice boys and girls, would you please, tonight? I know you want to play, but wait for playtime. Teacher Dearest will be ever so grateful."

Charleston cackled and slapped his knee. "Yes, *ma'am*."

All but one student laughed. Meri laughed with them, aware of the loaded silence in the back row. He obviously wasn't amused at the rapport she had established with his classmates.

The class quieted again and Meri resumed her reading without a glance at Brew. Just as she knew he would, he broke the silence.

"Teacher Dearest, what are we reading?"

"The short story on page ninety-six."

"Can I go to the rest room before I start?"

"You *may*, Brew." The time bomb was ticking, she thought. Brew knew *can* and *may*. He also knew no one had to ask to leave class.

Meri heard the chains on his boots clink as he rose to his feet. He sauntered toward the door, exchanging an elaborate high-five with Charleston as he passed his desk.

"*¿Cómo estás, Don Hector Chamorro?*"

"*Perfectamente, Don Brew Brodrick,*" Hector replied.

Meri recalled that in Spanish, *Don* implied both respect and a certain degree of familiarity. Brew obviously wanted to make the point that he had special rapport here, too.

"Looking good, babe," she heard him say as he passed Arlene Ainsworth. Arlene, she surmised, would be running her hand through her red-gold curls.

Meri kept her eyes on her page. She felt a strong pang of jealousy that surprised and unsettled her. Envious of Arlene because Brew had thrown a compliment her way? That was so petty.

Brew was coming closer to her desk on his journey to the door. Picking up a pencil to keep her hands busy, she circled a key sentence that foreshadowed the climax of the short story.

"Marking up your schoolbook, Meri?" Brew murmured. "Tsk. Tsk. What will the book monitor say?"

"Very little, I'm sure," Meri replied. Paging back through the story, she underlined the sentence that signified the turning point.

"Want to join me in the little boys' room?" he inquired softly so that only she could hear. "We could play show-and-tell."

That brought her eyes up to meet his for the first time. He raised his eyebrows and strolled out the door.

In a few minutes, he strolled back in. For the remaining thirty minutes of class, Meri felt every slow slipslide of his gaze over her beige suit, down the front of her pink silk blouse. She sensed every assessing lift of his scarred eyebrow, every appraising tap of his forefinger against his cleft chin.

He lounged in his seat with his hands clasped behind his head and made lengthy surveys of her legs. Whenever she turned away from the blackboard, she saw his tongue slide back from between his parted lips.

Finally, mercifully, the class was over and everyone filed out, Brew among the first. Meri slumped into her chair when the door closed after the last student.

She kicked her shoes off, pulled the pins out of her hair and closed her eyes.

Show-and-tell. His insolence knew no bounds. He was everything she had suspected from his first *Yo,*

Merideth. He was surly, boorish, odious and insufferable.

Rough diamond, indeed! Tomorrow she would call Emmett and tell him she'd had it up to here with the beer "baron."

OUTSIDE IN THE parking lot, Brew considered his options. He could tell Meri he'd been an ass in class and he was sorry. He could zoom off on TNT since there was no law against looking and being obvious about it. He could post guard here to make sure she stayed safe between the classroom and her car.

He'd already noted that she had driven the new one that had been parked next to the Jug in her two-car garage. Jug. Stupid name. Not a zinger like TNT. Brew stroked one hand over the flames on the gas tank. First-class flames he'd painted himself. First-class bike he'd customized himself.

He'd stay and make sure she got from classroom to car safely. He'd just called Shannon to make certain she was home. He wished he knew for certain that Duke Doyle wasn't there with her. Where did single fathers find baby-sitters for fifteen-year-old daughters, though? Good luck.

Scrounge was the best kid-sitter Brew Brodrick could find. Shannon still hadn't forgiven him for not calling her downstairs until the sixth puppy had arrived. She'd watched the seventh squirming miracle's birth.

Whenever he thought of watching the mystery of life with Meri, he thought about being in love. He'd never been in love. Never in real, rose-scented, romantic love.

Brew sat back, cocked the heels of his boots on TNT's customized chrome handlebars, and settled down to wait.

Two minutes later he saw Meri come walking toward her car. Her hair was down and loose around her shoulders, pale and gleaming in the parking-lot lights. He noticed her slight misstep when she spotted him in the far corner of the lot. Her pace quickened.

He watched her open the car door, get in, slam it closed. Then, surprised, he saw the door open a split second later. She got out and marched directly to him. He slid his heels off the handlebars and sat up. He wished he'd put his helmet on. This looked like a showdown.

"You," she accused when she reached him, "owe me an apology right now. If I don't get it, *you* can forget my help on Friday and Sunday nights. You can forget keeping up with the class. You can forget graduating with them." She settled her hands on her hips. "It's all up to you."

"Apology for what?"

"Sexual harassment. I know it when I see it. You know it when you do it. If you don't, you should. Think about it."

"I already thought about it." Brew looked away from the accusation in her eyes. "I'm sorry, Meri. I was an ass in class."

"You were worse. You were—"

Brew held up a hand. "I apologize, all right? As sorry as Duke would be after I got through with him if he did that to Shannon."

"Thank you," she said, turning away. "I'll see you on Friday night."

"Your place or mine, Meri?"

She turned back. "Yours, if that's all right with you."

"Fine. Bring Trina if you feel like it. Seven pups told me they'd like to see her. So did Shannon."

"Seven?"

"Yeah. Every one of them a miracle." Brew saw her eyes soften after he said that. It encouraged him to add, "Five females, two males. It's always ladies' night at Scrounge's milk bar."

He held his breath, hoping his wisp of wit would make her smile. It did. He breathed again.

"Good night, *Don* Brew Brodrick," she said, and walked to her car.

"IS MERI BRINGING Trina or not, Brew?" It was five minutes to seven on Friday night.

"How do I know? She didn't say one way or the other when I mentioned it."

"You could have called and found out."

"I didn't have time."

"She'd better bring that munchkin," Shannon said. "I did all my homework early so I could show my face outside my room tonight."

"Do homework early every night and your grades might look better at report-card time."

"Oh? How did yours look when you were my age?"

Brew glowered at Shannon over the vase of fresh pink roses in his hand. "You know what I was at your age. A dumb, no-good dropout in and out of juvey court every other day. Is that what you want to be?"

"School bores me numb, Brew."

"It bored me, too, but I wish I'd hung in there. I *really* wished it the two years I spent locked up. Stay in school, do the homework, get passing grades and you won't end up in jail like I did." He handed Shannon the vase. "Put these out there for me, would you? I'll go down and turn on the lights."

Shannon didn't move. "Meri hasn't even rung the bell yet."

"It's dark down there," Brew muttered, checking his nails for any specks of white. They'd painted the living room walls on Thursday morning. "She might be early."

"You've got it bad for her, don't you, Brew?"

"What if I do?"

"Don't get so defensive. You've been single a long time—for a man. You and Meri and Trina and I could be a neat family." Looking pleased at that possibility, she pushed through the swing doors.

Brew shoved his hands in his pockets. His daughter—fifteen going on thirty-five.

"Are we there yet, Mommy?" Trina strained against her seat belt to see through the windshield.

Meri pulled over to the curb in front of The Last Detail. "We're there. Sit still while I get my books."

"Where are the puppies?"

"Inside."

"Where the big long lights are?"

"Yes."

"I see Brew, Mommy."

Meri saw him through the passenger window as she leaned over to release Trina's seat belt. He was coming through the open door of the shop, thumbs hooked in the front pockets of his black jeans. His T-shirt was black. He looked like midnight, like danger, like sex itself. Midnight—the hour of dreams.

"Be a good girl tonight, Trina," she murmured, adjusting her daughter's peppermint-stripe jumpsuit.

"You be good, too, Mommy."

"We both will. Wait for me to get out and come around." Meri turned to her left and found Brew at her door.

"I'll take your books," he said as he opened it for her.

She gave them to him and slid out, trying not to show too much thigh below her knee-length slim skirt. A hot glint in his eyes told her he appreciated what he saw.

"Hurry, Brew," Trina demanded. "I want to see the puppies."

"At your service, Miss Whitworth." Brew saluted like a chauffeur before he closed the driver-side door.

"Don't let her give you orders," Meri said, following him around the front of the car. "You'll live to regret it."

He snorted. "Shannon already taught me that. I learn it again every day." Without turning to look at her, he remarked, "You look nice in that gray-green color you've got on."

"Thank you." Meri smoothed her hand down the double row of buttons on her silk blouse. "You look nice in black, Brew."

"I wasn't fishing for strokes, but thanks anyway." He opened Katrina's door and handed her out. "Ready for tons of puppy love, Katrina Denise?"

"Lots and lots. Can I ride on your shoulders?"

"You bet." Brew handed Meri the books and swung Trina up. "Duck your head going through the door."

Arms in a stranglehold around Brew's neck, Trina giggled with delight and ducked. Meri followed them into the shop where Brew reset the burglar alarm.

"You've got lo-o-ong hair," Trina informed Brew. She held a fistful of it straight out from his scalp as she rode his shoulders through the shop. "Wow. Like a rock star."

Meri warned, "Trina, don't pull."

"I didn't, Mommy. Did I, Brew?"

"Nope. You comfortable up there?"

"Yes. But where's the *puppies?*"

"Right here," said Brew, coming to the foot of the stairs. A big packing box had replaced the beanbag pillow. Scrounge was nursing her seven offspring.

Trina let out a squeal. "Mommy, look! Look!" She clapped both hands over her mouth, her eyes round.

"Hey, Shannon," Brew called up the stairs. "Trina's here."

Instantly Shannon appeared in the open doorway. "Munchkin. What's up?" She took the stairs two at a time, fashionably adolescent in red leggings and an oversize sweatshirt. "Hi, Meri. That's a great color you've got on. Like olive trees in the wind."

Struck by the rich imagery of the simile, Meri was reminded of the raindrop poem. "Thank you very much, Shannon."

Trina chafed her heels impatiently against Brew's chest. "Want down, Brew."

"Here, give her to me." Shannon held out her arms and Brew swung Trina down into them. "You guys go on up. I'll show this pipsqueak all about puppies," she said, settling Trina on her hip.

Meri went ahead of Brew up the stairs to the kitchen, her ear tuned to the conversation below.

"First off," she heard Shannon say, "you can't touch Scrounge's pups without getting her permission first. She has to smell you and decide you're okay. Okay?"

"Does Scrounge bite?"

"Not if you're nice, munchkin. Put your hand out. Let her smell. Dogs can smell ten times better than people."

In the kitchen, Meri stopped and turned to Brew. "Scrounge *won't* bite, will she?"

He shook his head. "Never has. Shannon mothered the last litter until they were weaned. Scrounge is more her dog than Joe's if you come down to it."

"I guess I shouldn't worry, then."

"Nope. That's the tricky part. Worrying when you should and not worrying when you shouldn't."

"You've learned quite a bit about parenting in a year, Brew."

"Not enough to stop worrying twenty-five hours a day, Meri. Want something to drink?"

"Nothing for me right now, thank you. We made time on the way over here to stop for hamburgers. *And* fries. *And* milk shakes."

He went to the fridge and poured a glass of ice water for himself. "How's your thesis going?"

"It's plodding along." In truth, it was at another standstill. *Dark Brew*, her romance novel, had crowded it out again today. Meri shifted her books from one arm to the other. Those dreams . . .

"Plodding? Sounds like you'd rather do something besides a thesis. What?"

"Nothing, really. Just—"

"Just what?"

"Oh, I don't know. Every once in a very rare while I wonder if I could write a novel. It's nothing I seriously consider, of course."

"Why not? Sounds reasonable to me, if you can write."

"Whether I can or can't, Gran wouldn't hear of it. Mansfields are never novelists—certainly *never* authors of popular fiction."

"Is she why you can't give it a shot?"

"She's part of it, I suppose," Meri conceded. "She took me in when I was orphaned, and made me feel accepted as a Mansfield. I owe her so much for her goodness of heart."

Brew's eyebrows rose. "More than you owe yourself?"

"Brew, pipe dreams and realities are two different things. If Mansfields bear a burden with their name, they also enjoy the privileges of it."

"So, what would you be without the burden, Meri? Underprivileged, or relieved?"

"It would be a relief," she admitted. "The weight is too heavy at times. If I were simply Meri Jones, for instance, I'd probably be writing fiction. But I'm not Meri Jones, am I?"

"Nope. You're just a Mansfield who's letting your family name and your grandma say what you can and can't be. Go ahead and write, why don't you?"

"I *do* write, Brew, every day. It takes a lot of writing to produce a thesis."

"Yeah, but that's not the real thing. What would you write if you were just yourself?"

Meri hesitated, took a deep breath, then replied, "Romance novels." Discomfited by revealing her secret and uncertain why she was unburdening herself to Brew, she shifted her books again. "Perhaps we should get started."

"After you," he said with a nod toward the swing doors.

Meri noticed two things as she passed from the kitchen into the living room. "Roses again." They caught her eye first. "You make a habit of them, I see."

Brew shrugged. "A hard habit to break, once you smell them."

Pretending puzzlement, she looked around the room. "Something seems different in here, but I can't quite..."

"We painted."

"Really? A different shade of white, is it?"

"You're supersmooth, Miss Manners, but I'm on to you. It was dirt-white before, now it's white-white, just for you. Have a seat."

Blushing at being so transparently polite, Meri sat on the couch.

"I feel badly that you've redecorated because I'm teaching you here, Brew. Fresh roses are expensive. They're—"

"Your favorite of all flowers," Brew cut in. "The main ingredient in your perfume. I know. That's why I didn't pass them up." He sat down next to her.

"You never made special efforts for Emmett."

"Emmett isn't a lady. You are. He doesn't wear cashmere. You do." Brew reached over and took Meri's hand. "His skin isn't like silk. Yours is."

"Brew..."

"Guess what, Meri?"

"What?"

"I reached over and touched you and you didn't jump out of your skin. Just look up and tell me you like the paint job."

Meri looked up. "I like the paint job. I love the roses."

"Have you ever held hands with a biker/brewer?"

"No, never."

He circled two of her knuckles with his thumb. "How does it feel so far?"

Meri didn't know what to say. She was amazed that she hadn't jumped and wasn't shaking. She felt the warmth of his hand, the hard texture of his callused palm. She wanted to move closer to him, but felt apprehensive about doing so.

"It feels good, Brew."

"Slide over here a little closer to me, Meri. I won't do anything you don't want. I promise."

Careful, cautious, Meri followed the gentle tug of his hand. She stopped before her shoulder could rest against his.

"Now," he said, "look up again. At me."

She did as he asked. "None of your lessons are getting taught this way."

"Teach me something else tonight, Meri. Teach me how to handle cashmere and silk. Tell me why I scare you."

Meri shook her head. "There are things I can't tell anyone. There must be things about yourself you could never, ever tell me. Aren't there?"

"You bet. I've got bedtime stories you probably can't even imagine. But I don't remember me doing anything X-rated Sunday night. Do you?"

"No." Meri decided to be frank. "I'm attracted to you, Brew. But I wasn't expecting it, and I'm not ready for it."

"Hey, I'm not pushing for the moon, lady. Holding hands. A hug because Scrounge did a great job the other night. A kiss, maybe, tonight. That's all. Kid stuff."

"We aren't naive children," she objected.

"Look, does this have anything to do with why your marriage hit the rocks?"

"Brew, you're asking questions I can't answer."

Brew tipped her chin up with his forefinger. "I'll bet you could answer to a kiss if we took it nice and slow."

Meri told herself that this was a man she'd begun to trust. Brew's eyes told her to chance it. His forefinger traced upward from her chin to her lower lip.

"You've been wanting to kiss me," he murmured. "You want to taste my lips. Don't be afraid, Meri. I won't do any more than kiss you. Not until you want more."

Meri almost nodded. For two weeks she had wanted to know if his kiss would feel and taste the way it had in her dreams, if the midnight magic could be real. His fingertip outlining her lower lip was real enough, magic enough. She leaned toward him and caught the scent of his skin and hair. Bergamot. It was her second favorite fragrance.

Brew cupped her cheek in his palm and drew her forward. Her way would be his way. This light brush of her lips to his, her way. The same brush of his own to hers, his way. The smallest press, the barest parting, the whisper of breath—hers and his together.

It was the sweetest contact he'd ever known—sensitive and vulnerable, petal-soft and romantic. It was the kid stuff he'd been deprived of too early in life. It was a first for the baddest boy in school.

"There," he said huskily in wonder when she pulled slowly away. "That wasn't so bad. Was it?"

Meri touched the fingers of his hand almost reverently to her lips, then shook her head. Footsteps sounded on the stairs. She loosened the near death-grip she had on Brew's hand.

He handed her a book from her stack on the coffee table and took a pencil and a pad of lined paper from his own pile. "What did I miss this week, by the way?"

"Mommy, Mommy!" Trina exclaimed, bopping through the swing doors. "Scrounge has titties!"

"Breasts, short stuff," Shannon corrected from the kitchen. "What kind of soda do you want, lemon-lime or orange?"

Trina called back, "Orange, please." Eyes round and awed, she held up ten fingers for Meri and Brew to see. "Scrounge has *this many* breasts. Lots more than you, Mommy."

"Eight more than you, Mommy," Brew mumbled, trying to suppress a grin at Meri's flushed cheeks and mortified expression.

Trina singled him out next and announced, "The boy puppies have tiny little penises."

"Just like you, Brew," Meri smugly rejoined.

"K.D., get your big mouth in here and help me," Shannon scolded. "Some words you shouldn't say in public."

"Like the F-word?" Trina inquired, pushing backward through the doors.

"*Never* say that one," Shannon replied.

Meri and Brew sat poker-faced, listening to their daughters clump down the stairs and out of hearing. Brew was the first to glance sideways. Meri's eyes met his.

He said, "Two is plenty."

She said, "'Tiny little' is quite sufficient."

They burst out laughing together and then settled down to work. At the end of the hour, Meri was frowning.

"I really can't understand why you're in this class, Brew. No errors in your spelling, nothing lacking in your grammar and reading skills. You certainly could pass the GED test and have your certificate without any class time. Have you considered taking the test again?"

"No. You see . . ." He hesitated, drumming his pencil on one thigh. "I cut a deal with Shannon a few months ago. *I* stay in school, she stays in school. *I* graduate, she graduates. Get it?"

Meri blinked. "This is all a—a charade?"

"What would *you* do in my shoes, Meri?"

"The same, I suppose," she replied after a moment's thought.

Brew spread his hands, palms up. "You're not wasting your time if she stays in school. Neither am I, since I need the diploma. I should have made a C average—part of the deal we cut. My mistake."

"That reminds me, Brew." Meri reached for a folder. She opened it and drew out the raindrop drawing. "The girls did some artwork the night you came to my house. Shannon did more than artwork." She handed it to Brew.

He scanned the drawing, read the poem and frowned. "Shannon did this?"

"It's quite special," Meri said, nodding. "If the poem is original, she has a special talent. Perhaps a true creative gift."

"A gift for pulling straight *D*'s is what she has." Brew snorted and tossed the drawing onto the table. "Duke Doyle is two of those *D*'s. You know what I find when I get home last Monday night? She's got a hickey she didn't have before I left for class." He pointed to one side of his Adam's apple. "Right here, she's got a beaut. Guess who had company while I was gone?

"She swears a racquetball dinged her in phys ed that day. She thinks her old man doesn't know, but I've got news for her. He knows. He's sucked so many hick—" Brew stopped in midword, stunned by his fatherly tirade. He growled, uncomfortably, "Shut me up."

"I've seen 'dings' before, Brew," Meri said to put him at ease. "The more gifted a child is, the more precocious she sometimes is." Meri looked down and smoothed her skirt to avoid Brew's eyes as she added,

"She also knows you were quite sexually advanced at the same age."

Brew crossed his arms over his chest. "What do I do? Lock her in a chastity belt and throw away the key? Make sure she's never without a party hat?"

"Party hat?"

"Condom."

"Oh." Meri had to smile. "I keep forgetting that slang is your second language."

"When I get steamed, it takes over," he mumbled. "Sorry."

"Don't be. It's very descriptive. Poetic in its own way."

He barely quirked his lips in response. This wasn't the first time that Meri had seen frustrated parents of teenagers. A recent government survey she'd read had found that more than half of unmarried American women ages fifteen to nineteen were sexually active. Seventy-five percent of them reported having had two or more partners.

What was a parent to do in the face of statistics like that? What was a single *working* parent to do?

"You know what I should have done?" said Brew. "I should have cut a deal with her about sex, too. I don't do it, she doesn't do it. That's the way my life has racked up. You're my first kiss since she walked in the door last March. First. God's honest truth." He was silent a moment. "I'm your first, too, in a long time, from what I can tell."

Not knowing what to do with her eyes or hands, Meri awkwardly rose to her feet. "Sunday night? Same time, same place?"

"Whatever will keep Shannon in school," Brew replied, stacking Meri's books to carry out for her. He picked up the raindrop drawing. "Are you taking this?"

"Yes." She was going to have a private chat with Shannon on Sunday night. If the girl was gifted, she should be in special ed classes.

Brew, however, was a separate matter. Now that she'd kissed him, she wasn't at all sure what she'd do about *him* on Sunday night.

8

MERI WOKE EARLY ON Saturday morning with more dream material for *Dark Brew*. "I need you," Brew had whispered.

This time he had led her hands under his T-shirt to explore the thick hair on his chest, then drawn them down to the silver buckle of his black belt. "I need you all the way, Meri."

The dream kept Meri flustered, and feverishly writing more of *Dark Brew*.

That afternoon, after Matilda and Trina brought over a fresh batch of Santiago's cookies, Matilda shooed Trina out to play on the swing set in the backyard.

Meri came and stood beside her, watching Trina through the kitchen window.

After a moment, Matilda said, "You know how I feel about animals on the property, Merideth. A goldfish or a canary is one thing, but I will not tolerate a dog. Katrina saw these puppies last evening. Now she wants one as her Easter present next month. You might have considered that before you took her with you."

"The puppies are all spoken for, Gran. I explained that to Trina before we went to Mr. Brodrick's, and explained it again after we left."

"That's commendable of you, Merideth, but what am I to give her for Easter now? A puppy is the only thing she is requesting."

"How about giving her a stuffed-toy puppy, Gran?"

Matilda gave the suggestion several moments of grave consideration. "I hadn't thought of that. Perhaps I will. I must say, Merideth, the place she tells me you both visited last evening sounds highly unusual. Motorcycles everywhere, she says."

Meri nodded. "Mr. Brodrick restores antique motorcycles. He does highly specialized work for very serious collectors." She queried, "Didn't Malcolm Forbes collect antique cycles as well as Fabergé eggs before he passed away?"

"I'm not certain," Matilda replied. "You'll have to ask this Mr. Brodrick, since he's such an expert. An older man, is he?"

"His daughter is almost sixteen, I believe," Meri hedged.

"She must be the 'Shannon' Trina likes so much."

"Yes." Meri braced herself. Trina may have chattered on about more, including Shannon's manicure and Brew's past-the-collar hair.

"Have you heard from Emmett since last week?"

Meri relaxed. "He called just this morning. Complications of his fracture will keep him in the hospital longer than he first thought."

"Poor man."

Meri smiled. "Maybe not. He says he's fallen in love with one of his nurses. It sounds serious."

"Well, how very romantic. Spring skiing led him to love. Isn't that nice? However, you will now be substituting longer. Will the added teaching time interfere with your thesis schedule?"

Meri mentally crossed her fingers before she answered, "I'm squeezing everything in just fine."

"I do hope so. Mansfields have a reputation for punctuality. I hope it hasn't slipped your mind that I'm leaving at eleven sharp on Monday morning for Boston. The servants will be taking their vacations, as usual, and Ingrid's cousin, Elsa, will come to sit Trina the nights you teach."

"We'll miss you," Meri said, amused at the idea that any of it could possibly slip her mind. Matilda's Boston trip occurred every year in mid-March and lasted seventeen days. The servants always went on vacation then, too.

It was the only Mansfield tradition Meri had never found confining in any way; the only one that released her from Matilda's watchful eye. Though she would miss Matilda, she would enjoy more personal freedom.

"I'll miss you and Katrina, Merideth. At my age, it's a great comfort to have family next door. Come for breakfast before I leave, would you?"

MERI DROVE OVER to the shop on Sunday evening. Shannon and Trina were downstairs with the puppies, and Meri was settling on Brew's couch when the phone rang.

He went into the kitchen to answer it and came out a minute later looking mildly perturbed. "Problem with the brew kettle at the San Francisco pub," he said. "I've got to drive over and check it out."

"Oh. Well, we'll have to reschedule," Meri said. She stacked her books, unsettled by the disappointment she felt at having spent only a few minutes with Brew.

He grabbed his jacket and helmet from a kitchen-wall hook.

"That was short," Shannon remarked, looking up from Scrounge's box as they came down the stairs.

Brew explained about the phone call. "Get your jacket and helmet," he instructed Shannon. "You're coming with me so I don't have to worry about any racquetballs dinging you while I'm gone."

Meri looked at Trina, who cradled a puppy in her arms. "Give the puppy back to Scrounge, sweetheart. We have to go, too."

"Don't want to go." Trina's lower lip began to push out.

"Trina, this is no time to make a fuss."

Trina repeated loudly, "Don't *want* to go. I want to play with the puppies."

Glancing shrewdly from Meri to Brew, Shannon intervened. "Why don't *you two* go and leave us kids here to baby-sit each other? You can wear my jacket and helmet, Meri."

Brew looked at Meri and raised his shoulders in question. "Want to see where I work?"

"Well, I . . ."

"Go, Mommy," said Trina, making shooing motions.

"Good thing you wore pants tonight, Meri," Shannon observed, scrambling to her feet. "I'll get my stuff for you." She raced up the stairs before Meri could object.

"I get to sta-ay," Trina crowed in a victorious sing-song. "I get to sta-ay."

Brew shrugged at the exasperated look Meri gave him. "We're outnumbered ten to two. Seven puppies, one dog, two kids."

"That doesn't mean we have to go on your bike," Meri pointed out. "My car will get us there."

"You don't like TNT, Meri?"

Before Meri could reply, Shannon came galloping down the stairs. "Here you go. Everything you need." She draped her bronze-tone leather jacket over Meri's arm and tossed her helmet to Brew. "Show her how it works. Bye, guys. Have fun."

Meri found herself following to the rear door of the shop. Shannon came after them to reset the burglar alarm, and two seconds later, Meri and Brew were standing in a dark back alley beside TNT.

"Nice night for a ride," he said. "How does that jacket fit you?"

"I'm not sure yet." Meri put it on and got it zipped. "Fine, I guess." She reached for the helmet.

Brew held it away from her. "I'll do it. You were all thumbs the last time, remember?"

"That was also the *first* time," Meri reminded him. She tucked her hair behind her ears. "My first 'hog' ride."

Brew chuckled. "You did all right for a first-timer. Almost cracked my ribs with the hold you had on me, though."

"I did not."

"Did too. You were sure we'd crash."

"I'm still not certain we won't, Brew."

"Trust me, Meri." He trailed the fingers of one hand along her jawline. "I'll keep you safe."

For a moment Meri thought he was going to kiss her. She almost tilted her head to the proper angle for a kiss. The next moment, however, he lowered her helmet and fastened it, then donned his own.

He pulled a pair of gloves on, rolled TNT into the center of the alley, mounted the bike and started it. When he gestured for her to get on, Meri knew the routine. *Feet on the foot pegs. Scoot forward. Arms around him.*

"Too tight?" she asked over the roar of the motor.

"Tighter," he replied. "I was kidding about the ribs."

"How's that?"

"Good. You feel real good that close, Meri. Don't let go of me."

Lean when Brew leans. Keep your eyes open. He'll keep you safe.

Meri enjoyed the ride through Berkeley, Emeryville, and over the Bay Bridge into San Francisco. In the two weeks since she'd met Brew, her fear of him had lessened, her trust of him had grown.

Holding him in her arms was not the frightening physical contact it had been two weeks ago. Though it still wasn't second nature to her, she didn't feel frozen with apprehension. A big, strong man was a good thing to wrap oneself around during a bike ride.

The view of the city was spectacular from the Bay Bridge. She saw the Ferry Building, the Transamerica pyramid, Coit Tower. The Bay Area was her home, but she had never viewed it over the broad shoulders of a biker on a custom Harley.

Brew steered through a maze of side streets and narrow back alleys south of Market Street. "Shortcuts to work," he told her as he finally halted TNT in an alley near a rear-entry door marked Brews. "I know them all."

Meri didn't doubt it. The door opened into a huge space crowded with stainless-steel tanks. Just inside, Brew stopped her to remove her helmet and his. He hung both on the doorknob, took her hand and led her around the largest tank.

A glass wall sealed the tank room off from the pub area, which was packed with a Friday-night crowd.

"Hey, Brew!" someone called from above. "Up here." Two young men in coveralls were standing on a green steel platform that half circled the tank.

Brew squeezed her hand. "They're my assistants. Good at brewing but they got cocky tonight and may have screwed up. Stay put. I'll have a look." He climbed the short ladder that led to the platform and peered into a large opening on the side of the tank.

Meri saw him shake his head, then run one hand through his hair. "Too far gone," she heard him say. "Start over." The young men's shoulders slumped, and Brew gave them both a never-mind clap on the back.

He came back down the ladder. "Want a ten-step, eyeball tour of how beer gets born?"

"I'd love one."

He pointed at a big dome-topped tank. "First, that's where the malt is stored. Taking the tanks from left to right, the malt goes into that gristmill and gets cracked. Second, the crushed malt is mixed with hot water in the brew kettle where my two aces just burned a batch.

Third, the liquid is separated from the solids in the tank section above the kettle. Fourth, the liquid gets boiled in the section below the kettle. Are you with me, so far?"

"More or less."

He pointed to a smaller tank connected by pipes and valves to the one his assistants were tending. "Fifth, that tank removes the solids formed during boiling. Sixth, we run the liquid from there through a cooling process. Seventh, the hopped liquid is aerated and yeast is added in the next tank. Bored numb yet?"

"I think I can keep my eyes open through the last three steps. Which are . . . ?"

Brew pointed to a bullet-shaped tank. "Eighth, fermentation and maturation happen there. Ninth, the brew is filtered and yeast is removed. Tenth, we keg it."

Nodding as if she now fully understood the process from grist to keg, Meri said, "Be kind enough not to give me a pop quiz."

"Be glad I didn't pile on the brew lingo—mash, lauter, sparge, trub," Brew laughed. "There's a lot to this business."

The corners of his eyes crinkled and Meri laughed with him.

Brew looked down at her. "Want a beer?"

"Some other time, yes. I have to drive home when we get back."

"Were you warm enough on the bike? I have a sweater upstairs in my office."

She held up a hand. "I was fine. Really. I'll be fine going back, too."

"We should be doing that, I guess."

"Yes. You're through here?" Gazing into his eyes, she felt as if she'd suddenly run short of oxygen—she would soon have her arms around him again.

"I'm through here," he murmured, taking her hand again. "Let's go."

Outside, they donned their helmets and mounted TNT. Brew kept the engine at a slow idle for a moment and lifted her palms, first one and then the other, for the briefest instant to his lips. He replaced them flat on his stomach before she could react, then took off.

Meri felt those two separate kisses pulse on her palms that were flattened on his muscled torso. Shivery chills of sensation moved up her arms to the tips of her breasts. They made her think of everything he'd done in *Dark Brew*.

Nothing he'd done so far was even remotely similar to what Trina's father had done.

At the east end of the bridge, Brew turned north on the frontage road that paralleled the Eastshore Freeway. A saltwater tang sharpened the night air. Meri breathed it in.

"Want some tunes?" he called back to her.

"Sure." Music would be nice. She'd noticed a radio-cassette player built into the bike dash. Brew punched a button and Tone-Loc's seductive version of "Wild Thing" began playing.

In the circle of her arms he moved his upper body to the beat of the music. Meri moved with him. It was a bit like dancing. She hadn't danced at all for four years. She had never danced with a biker on a Harley. Seeing the white flash of Brew's smile in the rearview mirror, she smiled back. This was fun.

Brew turned off into a small, empty parking area. A row of benches faced the city across the bay. He cut the motor and set the kickstand but left the tape playing.

"This tape is like TNT," he said. "A custom job. Shannon dubbed my favorite tracks on it and gave it to me last Father's Day." He turned his head slightly. "You don't mind stopping here, do you? I've always liked this spot."

"It's lovely," Meri agreed, aware only of her arms still around Brew, of her hands pressed flat against his stomach, of the way he was still moving to the beat.

Brew placed his gloved hands over hers. "Let's warm those up for you."

"Wild thing," the singers chanted.

Meri sat behind Brew, her thighs cradling his, her cold hands warming under his, searching for something to say. "What else is on the tape?"

"Some Stones, INXS, an Aaron Neville song recorded live at Tipitina's. He's next after this. Want to dance?"

"Dance . . . Here?"

"Sure." Brew swung one leg over TNT and stood. He slid Meri's helmet off and hung it on the handlebar. He added his to it, took off his gloves and held out his hand to her. "Leg over, Meri."

Brew was already swiveling his hips to the rhythm. Taking his hand, Meri got off the bike. The song was a relatively fast one. What could happen?

He gave her a playful fifties-style twirl to the right, first, then to the left. She laughed as the lights across the bay seemed to spiral and dip and sway as she moved to the music. "Wild Thing" faded away.

Then Brew slid his right arm around her waist and took her right hand in his left. "The next one's Aaron doing 'Tell It Like It is.'"

"I'm not sure I've heard of Aaron Neville," Meri said, sliding her left hand up to Brew's shoulder.

Brew assured, "You'll never forget him after this."

After the first few notes of the most liquid, evocative male singing voice she had ever heard, Meri knew Brew was right. He led her into a slow, swaying step that very gradually brought her body closer to his.

Aaron sang about love and longing, about telling it like it is, about honesty and devotion. The lyrics and music touched Meri's heart even as Brew's thighs brushed against hers. His chin fit against her temple, his hand curled over hers.

"Meri," he whispered into her hair. He dipped his head and kissed her cheek. His feet stilled. Pulling her close, he whispered, "I never thought I'd like you so much."

Feeling his knee nuzzle between her knees, Meri stiffened and her breath caught. "Brew..."

"Meri, I mean it." He lowered his hand from her waist to cup her hips close to his. "I like you so much. I want you so much."

"No." Meri felt her knees begin to quiver. "Please...don't...don't..." She pushed away and spun out of his hold.

"Don't be afraid," Aaron sang.

But she *was* afraid. Memory swamped her. She squeezed her eyes shut as Brew caught at her wrist. Flinging his hand off, she turned and ran. Away from his hard, male body. Somewhere. Anywhere.

The whine of a passing car on the frontage road forced her eyes open wide. A flash of headlights brought her to a stop. She'd almost run into the car's path. Running from whom? To where? To what?

Chest heaving, she covered her face with her hands.

Right on her heels, Brew spun her around by the elbow. "Stop, for God's sake!" He gripped her by the shoulders and shook her. "You have a death wish or something?"

"N-no." She shook her head and pressed her hands more tightly to her face. Tears squeezed out of her eyes. A sob pushed up out of her throat. Another followed it, then still another.

"Aw, Meri." Brew gathered her close and held her as she fell apart. "Don't cry," he softly pleaded. "I'm no good around crying, okay?" Feeling helpless, he stroked her hair. All torn up inside, he lifted her into his arms, carried her to one of the benches facing the water and sat down next to her.

"What's the story with you, Meri?" he asked when she quieted. "Please . . . tell it like it is."

Meri wiped her eyes and sat forward. "I had a bad experience a few years ago." She took in a deep breath. "I'm still getting over it."

"A bad experience like . . . rape, maybe?"

It took several moments before she could nod.

"I'd love to lay hands on him," Brew growled, "and tear him apart." He flexed his fists. "Where do I find him and pay him back for what he did to you?"

"You can't Brew. He's dead."

"Lucky for him." Brew's tone was hard with anger and frustration. "If he was alive, I'd rearrange him so he'd never touch a woman again."

Deeply moved by Brew's fierce protectiveness, Meri curled into the safe, strong curve of his arm. "I haven't been the same since. It apparently shows, if you've suspected the reason."

"I've only half suspected it was rape. The rest of the time I told myself it was because I'm not blue-chip, from your social circle."

Meri sighed. "For my grandmother it would be a class thing. For me, it's not. Not now that I know you better."

"Were you raped before, during or after your marriage?"

"Before."

"You weren't a virgin, I hope."

"I wasn't sexually active at the time, but I'd had two past relationships."

"You've said you never discuss your husband. Did he do it?"

"No."

"Who was it, then? Tell me what I need to know," he demanded softly. "Don't make me pull teeth for it."

"It was someone I knew before Alistair, a student at Turner High. He was killed in a street fight right after he attacked me. I—"

"I wish I'd been the dude who'd iced him." Brew flexed one fist again and drew her closer against him. "Go on."

"I went to England to recover," she continued, summoning the willpower to lie. "I met Alistair Whitworth there and married him. We divorced soon after Trina was born."

Brew fell silent, then said, "You left out the part about getting pregnant from the rape."

Meri covered her shock. She slowly turned to look at him and persisted in the lie. "Alistair was Trina's father."

"No, he wasn't." Brew shook his head. "You haven't recovered enough to make out with me tonight. So how did you make love with a husband back then? Plus, last week you slipped and said your grandmother was your Lamaze coach. It doesn't add up, Meri."

Meri bit her lip. "Please keep it a secret. Emmett knows I was pregnant before I left, but only Gran knows how and why. She arranged it all—England, a sham marriage, a divorce. I promised her that no one else would ever know."

"She must have a cool head. Money helped too, I'll bet. Lots of it to cover up an illegitimate kid."

"Brew, please. Promise me for Trina's sake."

"My lips are sealed," he assured her. "You're lucky she looks so much like you."

"I wish her temper were more like mine. As it is, it's more like her father's. Or perhaps it's more like *my* father's. She doesn't take no for an answer."

"Do I remind you of her father, Meri? I must, from the way you looked at me that first night."

"At first you did, a little bit. He was a gang leader, very troubled." Meri pushed her hair back from her face and stared across the bay. "I thought I could help him straighten out. I was going to be a do-gooder

Mansfield and change his warped life for the better. He changed mine. I was a naive fool."

"Yeah, you probably were," Brew agreed. "Kids can be hard-core bad enough that no one gets through to them. I walked to my own beat through the streets, so I know. Never raped anyone, though. Keep that in mind."

"I'm sorry about the way I've been, Brew. I know you've been confused by my behavior. I want the closeness I feel with you, but I'm afraid of what follows. Besides, we come from such different backgrounds."

"Yep. Blue blood, black leather. Debutante, delinquent." He was silent a moment, then reached over and took her hand in his. "None of it makes me want to skip your classes." He pressed her palm to his lips as he'd done earlier. "*I'm* the naive fool."

"No." Meri twined her fingers with his. "I've encouraged you in my own way. I've worn perfume, and dressed in colors I hoped you might like. I knew Trina would want you to stay that morning if I put the bug in her ear to make hot chocolate for you. I could have put my foot down against coming with you tonight, but I didn't. Something's happening for me with you. Perhaps I'm the one being foolish and naive."

"Perhaps I don't mind hearing you like me that much," Brew said, his voice husky. "Maybe I want to hear it again sometime. Like after a kiss, maybe. If *you* kissed *me*, would that be easier for you?"

"I'm . . . I don't know. Maybe we should just be getting back to our girls instead of—"

"Look, even a rape victim has to start again some-time. With someone. You could find worse 'someones' than me." He turned to face her and brought her hand to his lips again. "I won't move a muscle. Just my mouth, just a little. Then we'll go home."

Tentatively, Meri leaned toward him. It *was* easier being the one in control. She touched her lips to Brew's and felt his part slightly. Raising her hand to his cheek, she pressed her fingertips against the stubble of his beard. She could feel him breathe in through his mouth, creating a tender suction that brought her leaning all the way into his waiting arms.

"Show me you trust me, Meri."

She let the tip of her tongue slip between his lips. She had done this with him in her dreams, just this way, with darkness all around and the hot silk of his tongue luring hers. He tasted male and wonderful. He tasted like a man she could trust . . . and love.

Brew had never let a woman take the lead at the be-ginning. Except for Tessa. It was new for him to court the tender foray of a French kiss and then hold it, just hold it. It was an effort—a costly one he made for Meri.

He would be the one, he vowed; the only one to lie down with her and please her and bring her to life as a woman again.

Slowly Meri detached her lips from Brew's. She searched his face, indistinct in the darkness. "Was that better than before?"

"Only if it was better for *you*, Meri."

"It was, Brew."

He grinned, teeth flashing white in the night. "You'll have to try it again sometime."

THE GIRLS WERE IN Shannon's room when Meri and Brew got back home. Trina was perched on a chair and Shannon was kneeling in front of it, painting Trina's toenails every color of the rainbow.

"A piddycure, Mommy," Trina said when Meri came through the doorway.

"I see that." Meri sat down on Shannon's bed to watch. "What else have you been doing while we've been gone?"

"Making pictures and pomes. Shannon made the pomes."

"It's pronounced po-ems, short stuff," Shannon corrected. "Say it right."

"Po-ems."

"That's better." She looked up at Meri. "Where's Brew?"

"On the phone to the San Jose pub. Just checking in with the brewer there." Meri looked around at the rock-star posters on Shannon's walls. The only ones she could identify were Madonna and Prince. "Where are the pictures and poems you two made tonight?"

Shannon pointed. "Behind you on the bed."

Meri looked back and saw an untidy pile of papers. Picking them up, she leafed through them. Trina had done her best to draw puppies with whiskers, little black noses, and puppy-dog tails. Shannon had written two four-line stanzas of poetry. She had crossed out certain words and written in others. The rough draft read:

Laughing, the raindrops
Dance across rooftops,

Giggle down gutters,
Trip over shutters.

Sparkling, the raindrops
Smile on girls' topknots,
Garnish the grass
With jewels of glass.

"Shannon, these lines are lovely. Are they original?"

Shannon looked up, nail-polish brush poised in the air. "If you mean did I think them up by myself, sure. Why? Pretty bad, huh?"

"No, not at all. In fact, I was so impressed when Trina showed me the raindrop picture you did at our house that I saved it. I've been wanting to talk to you about it. Do you often write poetry?"

Shannon shrugged. "Not unless something sets me off. This time it was rain."

"You have an entire poem here, Shannon, if you add the one at my house to the end of this. This is quite a gift you have."

"*I* get a gift at Easter from Great-Gran," Trina put in.

"Stay still, munchkin." Shannon dipped the brush in the polish and finished Trina's last toenail. "Now, don't move until I say you're dry." She capped the nail polish and came to sit with Meri on the bed. "Me, gifted? No way." Almost defiantly, she added, "I'm a *D* student."

"Looking at your poetry, Shannon, I have to wonder why your grades aren't higher, at least in English."

"School bores me."

"It worries your father that you don't do better."

"He's always worrying about me. What I'd like to do is drop out." Shannon flopped back on the bed and stared at the ceiling. "Just drop out and forget school."

"Have you shown your English teacher any of your poetry?"

"Are you kidding? He's a jock. The only reason he's a teacher is to coach sports. *D* students get the real cream of teachers, let me tell you."

Meri had been an educator long enough to know that Shannon was right. At Meri's job interview at Turner High, the principal's first question had been, "Can you coach?"

She had expected to be asked, "Can you teach?" She never was. Fifteen years of tennis lessons and being a Mansfield had gotten her the job.

Bored. Meri knew it was a common adolescent complaint. If Shannon was creatively gifted, her present curriculum would certainly not interest her. She wondered how Shannon would score on assessment tests.

"You always look so nice." Shannon touched the sleeve of Meri's blouse. "If someone asks me to the junior prom, do you think you could help me look for a dress?"

"Why, yes. I'd love to."

"Promise?"

"Certainly. Who are you hoping will invite you?"

"Duke. Who else?"

"Will your father approve, Shannon?"

"I'll worm around him somehow. What's he doing out there? Getting *D*'s, like me?"

"*A*'s are more like it," Meri replied. "He's a very good student."

"He wasn't when he was my age."

"Am I dry?" Trina whined.

Shannon gave the polish a close look. "Not yet."

"When you're dry," Meri said, rising from the bed, "we'll leave. I'll go get my books together. I hung your jacket and helmet on the kitchen hook, Shannon. Thank you for loaning them."

Shannon sat up. "Did you have fun?"

"Yes. It was a good night for a ride." Meri turned to hide the flush on her cheeks and left the room.

Brew was hanging up the phone when she joined him in the kitchen. "I smell polish all the way out here," he said. "What are they doing?"

"Pedicures. Nothing harmful." She pulled out a kitchen chair and sat down. "I'd like to talk to you about Shannon."

"What about her?" Brew sat, too.

"The poetry she writes is exquisite. I've just read more. She may be gifted, Brew."

He shook his head. "No one with straight *D*'s in school is gifted, teach. Even I know that."

"Boredom with the ordinary curriculum is often a clue that a child needs accelerated courses. She may be gifted in other subjects, too."

"Her problem is attitude," Brew countered. "I know because I had one most of my life. It held me back. What's left of it still does, sometimes. If I changed mine, she can change hers and do the work her teachers give her. She can stop wanting to drop out because I'm not going to let her."

"Brew, I think she should be tested."

"I think she should straighten up. Kids with a lot less on the ball make C's. There's no reason Shannon can't."

Meri frowned at him. "She writes masterful poetry for her age."

"What if she does? Rhyming words won't make a living for her when she grows up. It won't pull in a paycheck like something practical will. She'd be better off learning to brew beer."

"If she has a gift, Brew, it should be identified and developed. She has every right to fulfill her potential and be what she wishes to be."

Brew raised an eyebrow. "Like you're fulfilling your wish to write novels, Meri? Rag me about my daughter's potential when you start developing yours."

Stung by his accurate aim at the weak spot she had so unwisely exposed to him, Meri sat for several seconds in tense silence until Trina skipped in, shoes on and sweater in hand.

"Shannon's doing a manicure now," Trina advised. "She says bye."

Brew pushed his chair back and stood. "I'll get your stuff."

Meri helped Trina into her sweater and lifted her into her arms for a big hug. "How's my little snuggle bunny?" she murmured, nuzzling Trina's blond curls.

Walking back in with Meri's books, Brew heard the words and saw the loving nuzzle. He met Meri's gaze. She frowned at him, unwilling to let their argument die.

Dammit, he thought as he followed her down the stairs. *Damned if some snooty, touch-me-not teach is going to tell me my daughter's a genius. Me, a dropout with a poet for a kid? Get real, Meri!*

9

MERI DIDN'T EXPERIENCE her usual feeling of freedom when Matilda left for Boston the next day. Brew had hit uncomfortably close to home with his rebuke that she should explore her own potential before worrying about Shannon's.

That day, Meri printed out what she had written of *Dark Brew*. She tried to imagine herself completing it as a novel and submitting it to a publishing house. That would require flouting Mansfield tradition and being herself. It would require defying Matilda.

The only Mansfield ever to do such things had been her father, Curtis, Jr.

Meri sat back in her chair, holding the pages of *Dark Brew* against her heart, wishing that she had known her parents.

All that she really had of Curtis and Taffy was their Reno marriage certificate and her birth certificate. Taffy's maiden name was listed as Smith on both documents, her parents indicated unknown. Nevada law wasn't particular.

She also had the only known photo of Curtis and Taffy together, a snapshot of them on the beach at Half Moon Bay. Matilda had presented it to her on her fourth birthday, along with the two certificates.

"It's all I have of their life together," she remembered Matilda stating on that occasion. "It's most of what I know of their life together. Your father and I were not on speaking terms when he married. But he was my son, you are his daughter, and that is that."

By the age of four, Meri knew "That is that" meant the subject was closed and locked. Treasuring the discovery from the photo, that her mother had been as blond as she, Meri had kept her questions to herself.

SETTING *DARK BREW* ASIDE Monday afternoon, she worked extra hard on her thesis. She tried not to think of how much she could add to *Dark Brew:* the bike ride last night, the brewery, the kiss, Shannon's poem, Trina's pedicure, the argument with Brew.

It was safer to work on the thesis and prepare lesson plans for tonight's class. There was no telling what Brew's mood would be. With him, anything—or nothing—could happen.

She wasn't expecting him to phone before class that evening, but he did.

"Still mad at me?" he asked.

"A little. Are you still mad at *me?*"

"A little. Would you like a bike ride to school tonight, anyway?"

A ride? Gran was gone. Ingrid's cousin was coming to sit Trina. There was nothing in the world to prevent a ride with Brew on TNT. *A ride. A truce.*

"Why, yes. I'd love one."

"Okay. Dress warm. I'll bring Shannon's helmet for you."

Meri dressed in wool pants, a sweater and a ski parka. She was waiting on her doorstep when he drove up.

As he secured her briefcase to TNT, he searched her eyes. "We need to get you a leather bike jacket."

"I'll put it on my grocery list, Brew." She gave him the smile he was searching for.

"Get on and quit kidding me, teach."

Laughing, she got on TNT behind him. Like an old pro, she settled in and hugged close. All the way to the school, she savored the solid strength of his body against hers.

He sat in the back row and said little in class. Meri wanted the session to end before it even began. She wanted to get back on TNT with Brew and go a little berserk with him tonight in Berkeley. For seventeen days Matilda would be gone. Gone!

Finally, class was over.

"Where to? Home?" Brew asked before driving out of the parking lot.

Meri shook her head. "Not yet for me, unless you have to get home right away."

"Want to go someplace and...dance, talk, whatever?"

"Yes. Someplace with a view."

"I know a better view than last night's."

The view was incredible. He took her to an off-the-road lookout high in the East Bay hills. Vistas swept in all directions, north to Marin, west to the city, south to the peninsula, east to Danville. There, on the top of the world, she sat in the saddle behind Brew and watched a full spring moon rise over the scene. Taking her helmet off, she shook out her hair.

Brew took his off, too, and settled back in the circle of her arms. "When I was in prison reading about your debut and all, I fantasized coming up here with a debutante on my bike. Weird how it's come true."

"How did you land in prison?"

"I hitched a ride with a friend. He had a truckload of rental cars he was hauling up to Seattle. I suspected before I hopped into the truck that they were hot property, but it was a free ride up north. I figured his business was his business. I lived risky back then.

"Anyway, we got stopped by the state patrol just outside of Redding and I got nailed for being an accomplice. With a juvenile justice record five miles long, I didn't get far with the truth. I pulled two years."

"You weren't really guilty, then."

"I was guilty of enough before that to pay for it with that bad rap. Justice equals out every once in a while."

"Where are your parents?"

"Dead. They overdosed on the same needle when I was seven. I'm an orphan like you. They had nothing to leave me and no one to leave me to, so I got to be a ward of the state. I was already no big believer in Santa Claus or the Tooth Fairy. I got worse with every group home and foster home."

"I'm sorry, Brew."

"Don't be. That's life."

"I try to think that when I visit my father's grave. I have no memory of him or my mother. Her body was never recovered."

Softly, Brew said, "I'll bet she was blond and beautiful, just like you."

"The only picture I have of her isn't very distinct," Meri said, blushing at his compliment, "but she *was* blond. No one came forward claiming to know her after the accident. My parents' surfer friends knew very little about her. They said she had mentioned running away from home at twelve, but she never told anyone where home was."

"Maybe she never had one," Brew said. "Like me. There are thousands out there like that. Coming from nowhere, going nowhere. Maybe your father was a bright spot in her life. Like Shannon and you are in mine."

"A bright spot? I am?"

"Yeah. You are. Want to make something of it?"

"I'm just surprised . . . and pleased, Brew. Actually, you brighten my life, too. I was thinking that all day today."

"While you were doing what else?"

"Working on my thesis, of course. That's why I'm taking leave from teaching full-time, after all. What did *you* do all day?"

"Couple of things. Brewed beer, for one."

"What else?"

Brew was slow in replying. "Spent a couple of hours on the phone with someone I called."

"It must have been important to take so long."

"Yeah. It was. You see, I—I called a rape counselor, Meri."

"Oh." Meri pulled away, feeling threatened by whatever he might say next. The more he knew about what she'd been through, the more he'd expose her deepest wounds.

"Don't tense up, now." He caught her hands and held them flat against his ribs. "I didn't tell the lady who I was or who'd been raped. I just asked a lot of questions."

She could barely speak. "What questions?"

"I asked how rape affects a victim. How it affects a victim's relationships with men afterward." He paused. "How a man should come on to a rape victim without reminding her of what happened to her."

Meri sat silently behind him, caught off guard and touched by his concern. His hands on hers were warm and reassuring, yet she felt uncertain and tentative.

"Maybe I shouldn't have called," he said, doubt rising in his voice. "You're feeling pressured, aren't you? A minute ago you were loose and laughing, and now you're wound up tight."

"You've taken me by surprise again, Brew. I didn't anticipate this kind of concern from you."

"You're wishing I'd mind my own business, aren't you?"

"No," she said slowly. "I'm grateful, but—"

"Look, I'm not putting any pressure on you. I just wanted to get close to you—to your heart—without scaring you."

"My heart?"

He nodded ruefully. "I'm making a mess of this."

"No," Meri told him, her heart filling with emotion. "You're helping me to feel closer to you than ever before." She relaxed against him as she spoke.

"That's what I want, Meri. To help." Brew's tone was earnest, intense. "I see red, knowing what that rape did to you. I want to turn it all around and make it right."

Drawing a deep breath, she asked, "What did the counselor say about how you should come on to me?"

"She said I could try letting you take the lead. She said you would if you're ready. If you are . . . so am I."

Meri felt overwhelmed by the knowledge that Brew's feelings for her ran this deeply. So deeply that he'd called a counselor for information and advice. She tightened her arms around him.

"You're quite a wonderful man. Do you know that?"

"Only because you bring out good things in me, Meri. It beats me how you do it, but you do."

"You bring out good things in me, too, Brew. Things I haven't felt in so long. Even so, I'm not sure I'm ready for this."

"Want to dance again? I brought another tape." He turned a key and punched a button. The Pointer Sisters came on, singing "Slow Hand."

"Oh, Brew," she breathed. "I love that song." She slid her hands up his ribs to his chest and felt the texture of the hair hidden under his white T-shirt. "But I don't want to dance to it." Her fingers fanned out over his collarbones. This was Brew. This was *his* body. *His* broad, muscled chest. No one else's. "I just want . . . to touch you."

"I'm the last man to turn down an offer like that, Meri."

Pressing her cheek against his back, Meri drew in the scent of his hair and his jacket. She heard the beat of his heart and how it quickened when her fingertips slowly mapped his chest and grazed over his hard nipples. She felt her own nipples peak against him in response.

He shifted his hips to the cradle of her open thighs. The bike rocked. "Babe . . . babe," he murmured, touching his fingers to hers to guide them over the nubs on his chest. "I like that."

"Slow hand," the Pointer Sisters crooned.

Meri let him guide her lower, rib by rib, to his waist. He lifted his hands and let her haltingly trace the shape of the buckle on her own.

"Touch me. It's okay," he reassured her in a velvet whisper.

Holding her breath, Meri ventured both hands lower over his pockets to the grooves of his thighs. Her thumbs fit perfectly there as her fingers splayed out over his muscular legs.

"You're so strong, Brew."

"Yeah?" He stroked his hands over hers. "Tell me more. Your breath feels good in my ear."

"You're smart . . . and handsome."

"Street-smart. That's about all."

"You're sexy."

"Now you're talkin'."

"You're not half as *bad* on the inside as you look on the outside."

Brew half turned in her arms. "You want me to dress preppy instead of biker?"

"No." She glided her hands up his chest once more, then added, "I've grown quite fond of your leathery black exterior."

"I've grown quite fond of the way you're treating it."

"Easy touch," the Pointer Sisters coaxed.

"Brew . . . if I did touch lower . . ."

He twined the fingers of his right hand with hers and led her hand down to his waist again. "Take your time getting familiar.

"I'm your fresh start here, Meri. I'm at your mercy." He lifted his hand from hers. "Walk your fingers any- where."

Haltingly, Meri traced Brew's rigid contours, then laid her open hand over his bulging fly and let it rest there. "This seems very unfair to you, Brew."

He laid his hand over hers. "What happened to you wasn't fair. It was a crime. I want you to feel safe with my body. And someday when you're ready, I want you in bed with me." Lifting her hand to his lips, he kissed each of her fingertips.

Meri knew then that she would be ready—not to- night, but someday soon.

"Brew, would you turn around and face me?"

He punched the tape player to Rewind, then swiv- eled and eased one leg over the saddle. He draped her thighs over the tops of his for comfort. "Like this?"

"Precisely." She framed his face in her hands and kissed him. She put her heart into kissing him. She made a soft, eager sound of invitation for him to taste her. He did, as his tongue glided past her lips and teeth.

"Slow hand," the tape began crooning again.

Brew pulled the zipper of her parka down. She pulled away and looked at him questioningly. He saw the spring moon reflected in her uncertain gaze.

"I only want you to feel what you make *me* feel," he whispered. "Only the good stuff. You're in control. I can stop on a dime if you say so."

Meri closed her eyes. Her emotions were in turmoil. She felt Brew's fingers smooth over her button-front sweater. They drew sensual patterns down her throat, then curved very lightly over her breasts.

"Are you truly an A man?" she whispered, trembling with a mixture of apprehension and anticipation.

"All the way." Brew moved his thumbs around the peaks of the small, soft mounds his palms cupped. He smelled Meri's perfume and knew he had to see what he was touching. First, though, he had to have her mouth again. He nibbled on her chin and murmured, "Kiss me, Meri."

She kissed and didn't stop, couldn't stop, as button by button Brew opened her sweater. Her heart was pounding, her flesh was heating, Brew was releasing the catch between the cups of her bra and—ah!—there was his warm, callused touch. No man had touched her in such a long time.

Brew pulled back and looked at Meri. He saw at that moment why moonlight and roses were symbols of soft-focus romantic fantasy. He could see every reason why certain roses were named American Beauty. The softest cry came from Meri's throat as he gently teased her taut, rosebud nipples with his thumbs. A cry of fear? Of pleasure?

"Tell me," he prompted, stilling his caress. "More?"

"Both, Brew. I don't know . . . I—"

"You're beautiful, babe." He moved his thumbs again. "I thought so the first time I saw you. More, or no more?"

"More . . . Just a little . . . Ohhhh."

Brew skimmed his lips over her jaw and down her throat. In the hollow at the base of it, he circled his tongue and tasted her perfume. He imagined her stroking the scent onto her pulse there just for him. He imagined being the only man in her life, the only one to hear her sigh in pleasure as she had just now.

His blood was hammering through him now, hot and insistent. His need was accelerating, but not out of control. He wanted to kiss Meri hard and deep, and lower his mouth to her nipples. He wanted to come on to her in a big way. He had to stop before he did anything that might scare her.

After tonight, he wanted her to remember the pleasure she was feeling now. He would be there with more later.

Regretful but determined, he fastened the catch of her bra. He buttoned her sweater and pushed the hair back from her face.

The Pointer Sisters were still singing into the moonlit night as he told her, "Next time, it's going to feel even better."

AT HER DOOR, BREW pulled Meri close and said, "Remember when I thought you were just a stuck-up deb?"

Meri smiled up at him. "Remember when I thought you were just a 'rude dude' on a 'hog'?"

"We're a pair for the books, aren't we?" he murmured. "Maybe for the ones you wish you could write?"

She thought of what she'd recently written—and shelved. "Maybe."

"Why don't you write one, Meri?"

Her only defense was to probe one of his major weak spots.

"Why don't *you* agree that Shannon should be tested?"

After a measured pause, he said, "I might...if you'd agree to write."

"What I should do is get inside. Trina's sitter must be wondering why I'm not in already."

"Be glad Trina's young enough for a sitter," he advised. "*My* daughter's probably getting another hickey. See you on Friday?"

"Yes."

"Here or there?"

"How about here for a change? The more Trina sees of the puppies, the more she wants one. Gran won't allow it."

"Kiss me one last time until I see you Friday."

Meri curled her arms around his neck.

She was dizzy—and happy—when he finally let her go.

THE NEXT MORNING, Emmett called.

"I'm in love with Nurse Alison Taylor," he said, "and I'm coming home this afternoon. Love heals."

"When do I get to meet Alison, Emmett?"

"She gets a vacation two weeks from now. I'll just have to limp alone down there until then. Not too difficult, since I'm in a full-leg cast. I can teach just fine sitting down. If you can hold the fort in class the rest of this week, I'll ease back into it with Brew on Friday and Sunday. How's he doing?"

"Quite well," Meri replied as calmly as she could. Her heart had just plummeted. No more Brew on Friday, Sunday and Monday nights? On the other end of the line, Emmett was silent, as if waiting for her to continue. Hastily, she added, "You should have told me he doesn't really need to prepare for the GED."

Emmett laughed. "It's a good man who'll do that to keep Shannon in school. You've already deduced that's why he and I—and you—make the effort."

"Speaking of Shannon, Emmett, I've discovered that she has an extraordinary gift for writing poetry."

"No kidding. Shannon?"

"Yes. I suspect she does poorly in school because she needs accelerated classes. I may be wrong, of course. Only special testing would prove or disprove me."

"Get her tested."

"I've already suggested it twice to Brew. He argues that her only problem is her attitude. Would you broach the subject with him? Try to persuade him?"

"Sure thing. Call him and tell him what's up and come see me for lunch tomorrow, noonish. You can fill me in on everyone and everything. I'll fill *you* in on Alison."

The phone rang again almost immediately after Emmett hung up. It was Matilda checking up on things.

"All is well there, I hope, Merideth."

"Yes, Gran. Good news—Emmett's coming home. He's taking his classes back next week."

"What about his special student? Are you free on those nights now?"

"Free . . . yes." How empty those nights would seem.

"I must say, Merideth, it eases my mind to know that. I didn't speak to you of it before, but Katrina described this Mr. Brodrick as having 'rock-star' hair. Moreover, her descriptions of his daughter's appearance were rather shocking."

Meri felt a flash of impatience. She snapped, "Mr. Brodrick and Shannon are honest and sincere. Who are we to judge their appearance?"

Her reply surprised her, for she never criticized Gran. She imagined Gran looking somewhat stunned in response, though not enough to halt the lecture.

"What sort of people allow their dogs to have puppies in this day of animal overpopulation? Seven, mind you. To be truthful, I've been quite concerned about you associating with such highly unorthodox, careless people."

"The Brodricks have been accepting of me, despite our differences in life-style and background, Gran. I've done likewise with them."

"Merideth, I've refrained from saying anything because you were doing a good deed for a friend, but some good deeds are going too far. You found that out four years ago. I would be greatly distressed if your poor judgment caused you injury again in any way. Surely you are aware of such concerns on my part."

"Yes, Gran," Meri replied, hauled abruptly into line by Gran's powerful reminder. "I appreciate everything you've done for me."

"You haven't been yourself lately, Merideth. Yes, I've noticed. I don't know what to make of your argumentative tone today. I have only your best interests at heart."

"I know you do." Arguing had been in vain. Gran was impervious, too set in her ways. To accept Shannon and Brew was too much to ask of her.

"How is your thesis proceeding?"

"Right on schedule, Gran."

"Good girl. And Trina? Does she miss her great-gran?"

"I'll put her on the line to tell you herself." Meri called Trina to the phone.

Depressed, she left Trina chattering to Matilda and moved to the front window to look out at the day. It had begun sunny and warm, but clouds were gathering. Meri knew that she had made too many missteps in the last two weeks to escape Matilda's sharp eyes and ears. Last night had been the biggest mistake. Fortunately, Matilda knew nothing of it.

Highly unorthodox. Careless. Such words both did, and did not, describe Brew and Shannon.

"Not at all people like us, Merideth," she could almost hear Matilda intoning.

Meri sighed and rested her forehead against the windowpane. For the past two weeks she had been getting more involved with Brew. It seemed now that she had lost some essential part of her Mansfield mind-set and demeanor in that time span. She had deliberately withheld specifics about Brew and Shannon from Matilda, knowing that Trina might reveal much of it anyway.

She had hoped that a child's ramblings would be given only half an ear up at the big house. She had been wrong. Now she tried to imagine herself going her own way, with Brew, as her father had done. She tried to imagine Matilda never speaking to her again. Or to Trina.

It was no easier to picture herself introducing Brew and Shannon at Sunday tea. *This is the man I'm falling in love with, Gran, and this is his daughter. He happens to be an ex-convict with a juvenile court record. He fathered Shannon with his foster mother and never knew the girl existed until a year ago. His parents? Heroin addicts. His address? The Last Detail.*

No. Brew might work two jobs to support his daughter and save for her future education, but he could never be included with people like the Mansfields, who lived orderly, exemplary lives from birth to death.

"Bye, Great-Gran," Meri heard Trina say. There was the sound of Trina dropping the receiver into the cradle, then the patter of her feet coming to the window where Meri stood.

"Mommy?" Trina tugged at her hand. "Can Shannon baby-sit me some more?"

No, sweetheart. Not anymore. Meri didn't say it. She said, "We'll see." Right now, she couldn't face one of Trina's tantrums. But she faced the fact that further association with Brew and Shannon would lead to insoluble complications. Ending it now would be best.

Meri held her tears back and called Brew at the San Francisco pub. She advised him of Emmett's good news.

"Thank you for your cooperation these past weeks, Brew. You've been a model student. Good luck as you continue with your GED studies."

Brew heard an unspoken rejection in Meri's formal tone. He tried to ignore it.

"We'll have to get together outside of school time, I guess. There's a beer-tasting here tomorrow night. Would you like to—"

"I'm terribly behind on my thesis," she cut in.

"Well, then, how about a movie next week?"

"I'm afraid not. With Gran gone and Ingrid on vacation now, it's difficult to arrange for a sitter."

He didn't need more than her vague replies to mount a counteroffensive. He'd been rejected most of his life. Damned if he'd give anyone on earth the chance to dump him before he dumped them. He didn't give a damn why she'd suddenly turned cool. He'd learned the hard way to never let 'em see you bleed.

"Yeah, well, I'm looking at a crammed datebook, myself. Too many babes, never enough time. You know how it goes."

"Yes," Meri acknowledged, aching inside. It was best that he'd taken the hint and ended what had no future. Far better for him to preserve his pride this way. "Goodbye, Brew."

Banging the phone down, Brew gritted his teeth. He'd known this was coming. She was a Mansfield. He was what he was.

He turned from the phone and rammed his fist against the nearest beer keg. *Cheers to you, too, Your Royal Piedmont Highness.*

10

MERI HAD LUNCH WITH Emmett the next day and kept it short, sweet and light. After signing his leg cast, she filled him in on the students' progress. He was pleased but preoccupied. Emmett was in love with his beautiful nurse.

"I'm going to marry Alison," he told Meri. "Two weeks and I'm as sure about that as I've ever been sure of anything. Let's all go out to dinner when she comes here on vacation."

"Yes, let's," Meri agreed, then fled before he could ask any more about Brew. Every mention of his name during lunch had caused her pain.

She picked Trina up from preschool and later that afternoon, during Trina's naptime, Meri sat down at the computer. She started typing her thesis and halfway through the first sentence she was in tears. She buried her face in her hands.

Brew. Memories of him were always intruding, no matter how busy she kept herself, no matter what she did. She knew her feelings now for what they were.

Dark Brew was more than a romance. It was a true story of love growing hour by hour, day by day.

She dabbed at her tears with a tissue and stared at the computer screen. Not one lifeless word communicated the love she felt, or the pain. She pressed the exit key, and then brought up *Dark Brew*.

Soon she was adding pages to the story, with loneliness and loss the theme where once there had been laughter and joy.

For the next week, the thesis took a back seat. Writing *Dark Brew* drove Meri day and night.

IN THE MIDDLE OF THE DAY, a week after Meri's lunch with Emmett, Meri had a surprise visitor at the carriage house.

"Shannon!" Meri opened the door wide to let her in. "What are you doing here?"

"Getting into big trouble if Brew finds out I came," Shannon said. "He doesn't know I'm here. He'd ground me for life if he did."

Shannon's hair and eyes were so like Brew's. "Why *are* you here, Shannon? Shouldn't you be in school?"

"I came to see Trina. I miss that short-stuff munchkin."

"I'm afraid Trina's at preschool. She'll be so disappointed that she wasn't here to see you."

Shannon shrugged. "Bad timing. I should have called, I guess."

"Now that you're here, can you chat for a few moments? I've been wondering if you've written more poetry."

"Some," Shannon replied, sitting down with Meri on the sofa. "I didn't bring it." She fixed Meri with her frank gaze. "What happened with you and Brew?"

"Nothing," Meri hedged. "Emmett is back, that's all."

"That's not all." Shannon shook her head in disbelief. "I saw lipstick on Brew's shirt when he got back from school last Monday night. The same shade you wear. I'm not color-blind. And his jacket smelled like rose perfume."

"Shannon..." Meri groped for words. "Your father and I come from different worlds. We—"

"That didn't keep either of you from falling in love."

"Brew and I aren't in love."

Shannon snapped the gum she was chewing. "Could've fooled me. And Trina, too. We were getting set to be stepsisters together."

"You were setting yourselves up for disappointment, I'm afraid. Adults don't fall in love in a matter of a few weeks. They—"

"Emmett did."

"Perhaps so, but Brew and I didn't," Meri attempted again, unable to meet Shannon's eyes.

Shannon countered, "Brew did. I've never seen him the way he's been acting. He bites my head off every word I say. Nothing I do is right. He used to be reasonable most of the time, but *now*..."

She rolled her eyes. "If he knew I was here, he'd ground me. He told me he would if I came here. That's how I know he's in love, okay?"

"If he disapproves, you shouldn't defy him by being here, Shannon."

"I miss Trina. I miss you, too. You thought my poetry was cool. And before you and Brew broke up, you promised you'd help me shop for a prom dress, remember?'

"I can't help if Brew won't approve," Meri told her. "You won't be able to attend the prom if you're grounded."

"Brew doesn't have to know you kept your solemn promise to me," Shannon argued shrewdly.

Caught by her promise and Shannon's adamant-yet-hopeful eyes, Meri sighed. "Very well. A promise is a promise. When do you want to go shopping?"

"Tomorrow after school. Can Trina come, too?"

Meri held up a hand. "Shopping with a three-year-old is impossible if you expect to get anything accomplished in less than eight hours. It'll be just the two of us."

Shannon nodded and smiled. "Like mother and daughter." Her smile faded. "Did Brew tell you about my mom?"

"He told me a little about himself and Tessa. He didn't explain where she is or why you came to live with him."

"Would you like to know?"

Meri hesitated. The more she knew, the closer she'd feel to Shannon—and to Brew. "I *have* been wondering," she found herself saying.

"Well, she's in Colorado," Shannon said. "My first stepfather who was with her when I was born walked out when I was a baby. He knew from my eyes that I was Brew's and not his. He used to beat her, you know. But that's her life history. She married another bouncer like him when I was six." Shannon sat silent for a moment. "Was your husband nice or a jerk?"

"Nice enough," Meri had to lie. "He wasn't abusive in the way you're describing."

"*Abuse* is the word," Shannon agreed. "After the second one split, Mom married a third one. I'd always thought Mom's first husband was my father until I found a picture of Brew stashed in the attic. I saw *my* eyes, *my* hair, *my* father. I showed it to Mom and she cracked. She told me the whole story then—how she couldn't have kids with her first husband and thought she was sterile. And how she and Brew . . . you know."

"Do you understand how that happened between your mom, an abused middle-aged woman, and a very young man?" Meri asked, concerned that Shannon *did* understand the combination of the need for tenderness, sexual desire and a stressful situation.

"Yeah. Brew explained it to me. After I tracked him down, he pretty much told me how it happened and why." Shannon looked up shyly at Meri. "My life hasn't been *Leave It to Beaver* or *The Brady Bunch*."

"No," Meri agreed, filled with empathy for the teenager and admiration for Brew's openness with her. "I'll be happy to take you shopping tomorrow. Our secret. When did Duke invite you to the prom?"

"He didn't. See, Emmett has this nephew, Ryan. It turns out he goes to my school. He's cute. He asked me. He's the first guy Brew's ever thought was decent enough for me."

"Things are looking up, then," Meri said. "I have a dental appointment in Walnut Creek early tomorrow afternoon. We could meet at Macy's if you can catch a bus from school."

"I'll be there," said Shannon. "Three-thirty. Front door."

SHANNON WAS WAITING, as promised, the following day. They couldn't find the right dress in any of the major department stores. They finally found it in a small dress shop on a side street.

Sapphire-blue satin with a poufy bow on the hip, it was a perfect fit except for the length. The shop, unfortunately, didn't make alterations.

"Would you help me shorten it when we get home?" Shannon pleaded. "Don't worry, Brew won't be there. He works later at the pubs now that Duke is history."

Meri let herself be persuaded. She'd had fun shopping with Shannon, sampling perfumes, looking at other clothing and chatting with her as they moved from one store to another in their search for the right dress. She was reluctant to end their time together.

They reached The Last Detail just after it closed for the day. Upstairs, Shannon changed into the dress and stood on the chair in her bedroom. Meri marked, cut and pinned the hem.

Meri was sticking the last pin through the blue satin when Brew's voice called from the kitchen. "Shannon? Where are you? Why aren't the dishes done? The kitchen's one hell of a mess."

"Omigod!" Shannon gulped. "What's he doing home?"

Meri was kneeling, her mouth full of pins, looking up into Shannon's saucer-round eyes.

Brew's heavy bootsteps approached. "What have you been doing since you got out of school?" he growled. "Didn't I tell you—" He stopped in Shannon's doorway.

"We went shopping," Shannon explained, stepping unsteadily down from the chair. "You're not good at it, so I asked Meri. It's my money. I paid for the dress."

His expression dark, Brew said, "You didn't ask my permission." He glanced from Shannon to Meri. "Neither did you."

Removing the pins from her mouth, Meri stood slowly. She handed Shannon a bathrobe that was draped over the chairback. "Put this on over your dress," she instructed Shannon, "and go check on the puppies. I hear one yelping."

"Good idea," Shannon breathed, slipping through the doorway past Brew.

"What's going on here?" Brew demanded when she was gone.

"I promised Shannon I'd help her shop for the prom when the time came," Meri replied. "She thought you'd be working late tonight. We were almost through pinning the dress."

"Forget whatever you were doing. The dress is going back. Shannon is *my* daughter. She needs something, I'll take her shopping for it."

"The dress can't be returned, Brew. We've just cut an inch from the hem. Aside from that, I'm merely keeping a promise. I'm not interfering."

"You took her shopping. You're here. No one said a word to me. I call that interference. Her behavior is bad enough without you encouraging her behind my back."

Meri stabbed the pins she held into the pincushion. "Her behavior," she retorted, "is symptomatic of her unrecognized need to develop her creativity."

"Develop your own before lecturing *me*, teach."

"I happen to have begun doing just that," Meri informed him. "I've written three chapters."

"I'll bet. Prove it."

"If I do, will you let me test Shannon?"

"Yeah," he said to her challenge. He turned up the collar of his jacket. "Let's see these three chapters."

"Now?" She took a step back.

"If they're written, teach, they're written *now*. Guess they aren't, huh? So forget testing Shannon."

"I'm not lying, Brew. They *are* written. They're just . . ." *All about you.* She needed time to edit what she'd written, to rework the chapters so he'd never guess he was the hero of the story.

"Like I said, forget testing. I told Emmett the same thing last week. Attitude is Shannon's problem. At-titude."

Realizing that this might be Shannon's only chance, Meri picked up her handbag and pulled out her car keys. "Let's go, then, Brew. A bargain is a bargain."

Brew followed her on TNT. He still wanted to be as near to Meri as he could get. He was ticked off at the way his heart was racing, even after she'd dumped him.

She doesn't want you, he reminded himself as he pulled into her driveway. *She's the one who called the whole thing off. You're not good enough for her, never will be. What do you care what she writes or doesn't write? What the hell do you think you're chasing after?*

"Elsa?" Meri called out upon entering the carriage house. "I'm home."

Trina skipped out of the kitchen followed by a matronly woman with a crown of gray-blond braids.

Immediately Trina crowed, "Brew!" An instant later, she was up in his arms, hugging his neck, tugging at his heartstrings with her effusive affection.

"Is Shannon here?"

"Not tonight." He was clearing his throat by the time he lowered Trina gently to her feet. He noticed that Meri had to clear hers, too, before she introduced him to Elsa as her "special student."

"Ingrid told me you are teaching some nights," Elsa said in a lilting Swedish accent. "Tonight also?"

"Yes. Mr. Brodrick and I have some, er, last-minute lessons to complete. Would you mind staying and taking Trina up to the big house for a short while? I'll phone you when we're through here."

"Very happy to, Miss Merideth." Elsa took the house key Meri handed her. "Come, Trina. We go make popcorn and watch the big TV in Mrs. Matilda's house. Yes?"

Beaming from ear to ear at that prospect, Trina willingly took Elsa's hand and left with her.

"I write in here," Meri said, leading the way to her study.

Brew followed her. He remembered kissing and caressing her in the light of the spring moon. Every kiss. Every caress. Moonlight and roses. His lips and fingertips tingled with the memory.

He sat in the chair Meri motioned him to, and watched her turn on her computer. Beeps and buzzes sounded as the screen lit. The room was small, lined with bookshelves that made it even smaller. He could reach out and touch her where she sat in her trim little typist's chair, tapping commands into the computer from the keyboard. Her hair was down tonight the way he liked it.

God, he loved her. He'd never been more miserable in his life.

"It'll take a few minutes to print out," Meri said, aware of Brew's gaze. She kept her own fixed on the pages feeding out of her new laser printer. Wishing she could shrink to nothing, she handed the first ten to Brew.

He began to read. After the third page, he took his jacket off. The printer stopped several minutes later. Riveted to what he was reading, he held out his hand for the stack Meri handed over.

"I'll be in the living room," she said. His eyes were racing over the words she had written and rewritten and poured heart and soul into, day after day.

Perhaps, she thought after she escaped, he would read only a few more pages and stop. When he didn't come out of her study after several minutes, she went into the kitchen and poured herself a glass of wine. Returning to the living room, she lifted it with trembling fingers to her lips.

Her deepest desires and fears were being exposed to the man she loved. She'd never been more miserable in her life.

In the study, Brew read all the way through to the last page. He stared into space, profoundly moved. Then, pages in hand, he came to his feet.

Meri was perched stiffly on the edge of the sofa, holding an empty wineglass in her hand. Brew sat down beside her and she stiffened even more.

"It's a love story," he said, husky wonder in his voice. "About us."

Meri managed to nod. She couldn't look at him, though, or speak. Was it really wonder in his voice, or was it mocking disbelief?

"Meri, look at me."

She slowly raised her eyes from their rigid focus on the empty wineglass. Then met his gaze.

"This relationship isn't over, is it?" he murmured.

"No, Brew." She struggled to find a stronger voice. "I was frightened by my feelings when I called you last week. I . . . still am."

Brew closed his free hand around her wrist. "Hey, babe. Mine scare me, too. You think it was easy for me to go as far as I got with you before you wished me luck? It was like biking without brakes, believe me. I never messed with love and romance until you. Before you, I was a take-it-or-leave-it, never-get-involved straight sex man. Nothing came easy for me with you."

"Even so, you don't have Gran to contend with, Brew."

"It's not just your grandmother turning your back on your story here." He shook the pages. "You got scared the day after I took you up on the hill. You knew we were headed for bed together. When you really thought about what that would mean, you freaked."

Meri pulled her wrist out of his tightening grip. "I had reason to panic," she said. "You know that you can make love without freezing up in fear. I don't know that *I* can."

"Wrong, Meri. I've never made love. Sex, sure, but not love. I come to you a virgin on that score."

"I might as well be in the physical sense. I'm more afraid now of lovemaking being painful than I was the very first time."

Brew set the papers aside and took her white-knuckled hands in his. "We'll stop if it hurts you, Meri. There are other ways to make love. You already wrote about some of them." Soothingly he drew her into his arms and held her.

Meri hid her face against his chest. "It's been so long," she said. "I'm uncertain of myself. I want to please you so much."

"You please me already, Meri. Trust yourself. Trust *me*. Have I ever given you anything to fear from me?"

"No."

He'd made their first kiss one of her most precious memories. Honesty, sincerity and genuine concern had prompted his call to the rape counselor for information and advice. He'd earned her trust in so many ways.

She slipped her arms around him and relaxed. "I know I have nothing to fear from you, Brew. I want you tonight."

He kissed her hair, her forehead, the tip of her nose.

"Take me into your bedroom, now, Meri," he whispered against her mouth. "Let me do what I did in your story."

She pulled slightly away. "I don't have anything for birth control."

"I do."

"Trina . . ."

"Phone the sitter," he murmured, rimming the shell of her ear with nibbling kisses. He stood, drawing Meri up with him. "Tell her you'll be an hour more here, maybe two."

Meri moved with him to the phone and dialed Matilda's number. "Elsa," she said, surprised that her voice didn't shake or break and give her away. "Mr. Brodrick and I will be longer here than I thought at first. Do you have any problem with keeping Trina busy for another two hours or so?"

"No problem," Elsa replied. "I am glad for the extra earnings."

"Thank you, Elsa. When Mr. Brodrick leaves, I'll call for you to bring Trina back."

Brew covered her hand on the receiver with his after she hung up. "Is the door locked?"

"Yes." Meri interlaced her fingers with his. "You've read my story, Brew. You know I'm in love with you and you know I'm unsure of myself."

"So? We're even."

She turned and faced him. "If I fail you . . ."

He shook his head. "You'd better give me the second, third and fourth chances I'd give you." He swept Meri up in his arms, honeymoon-style. "Where to?"

"Down the hall and to the right."

11

MERI WAS SURPRISED when Brew halted outside her bedroom and lowered her to her feet.

"Brew, what—?"

"Shh. Is the white eyelet-lace nightgown fictional or real?"

"Real . . . but wh—"

He hushed her with a sensual brush of his lips over hers. "Put it on and get into bed. Tonight your dreams come true." He nudged her into her room, then forced himself to close the door.

Returning to her study Brew took his time emptying his pants pockets and pulling off his boots, socks and belt. He pictured Meri undressing. Someday he would do that for her, but not tonight. He'd read the dream scenes she had written. He knew what she needed from him tonight.

He shrugged back into his jacket and moved the protection he kept in an inner pocket to a more accessible one. Then he sat down and waited several minutes more—a wait that seemed interminable.

In her bedroom, Meri lit a rose-scented candle and opened the door an inch before she slipped between her floral-print sheets. She felt breathless with anticipation and apprehension. What would he do? How would she react?

Meri had received only pleasure from his kisses and caresses. Would he receive pleasure from her, though? Would she ever be able to satisfy him the way a woman satisfies a man she loves?

Meri caught her breath as Brew slipped into her room and stood there, drinking in the sight of her. His eyes reflected the candlelight. The metal studs on his leather jacket reflected it, too, as he approached her bed and drew back the sheet.

She sat up against her pillows as she had done in every dream, watching Brew place one knee on her bed.

"I've come," he said in a husky whisper, "just for you."

Settling beside her, he drew his fingers down her throat to the pulse that beat in the hollow there. He circled his thumb-tip around the indentation and whispered, "Meri."

As his hand drifted lower to the ribbon ties of her nightgown, he kissed her and whispered other things— evocative suggestions and ravishing promises that made her heart beat faster and her breasts ache for his touch.

"I know what you want, Meri. I know why you love 'Slow Hand.' You've never had 'slow' like this before."

His chrome-blue gaze followed the unhurried journey of his hand. Leisurely he untied each silky ribbon on the low-cut bodice of her white eyelet gown until it fell open to her waist. He slipped his hand into the opening and cherished the delicate shape of her breast. He sipped a tiny gasp from her lips.

"You trust me, don't you?" he said gently, nuzzling the soft side of her throat. "You know I won't force you or hurt you?"

"Yes. I know." She sank down onto her side, drawing Brew with her. Pressing against the length of Brew's body, she kissed him deeply. Lacing her fingers into his, she returned his hand to her breast, inviting his caress.

Brew wanted her gown off. He wanted his clothes off. He ached to see her body and press his mouth to every inch of her skin. But he was giving tonight, not taking. He knew from the dream scenes she'd written that she needed special care and tenderness. He'd never been one to lie back and be taken, but tonight he would give as he'd never given. He brought her to lie full-length on top of him. She would dominate tonight. She had to know he was all hers.

He was that much in love.

Meri pushed herself onto her forearms above Brew to gaze down into his face. His body language communicated his message eloquently. His lean length was moving coaxingly under hers and his hands were sliding down the arched sweep of her back to her hips, yet he was making no demands.

No demands. No commands. No show of dominance or strength. She loved him for his restraint. She could feel his arousal against her belly. She could see need in his eyes. She saw, too, the wondering look of a man in love.

"I love you, Brew," she murmured, tangling her legs with his.

He gently drew her thighs forward to frame his hips. "Show me how much, Meri. Be my guide." He stroked the neckline of her nightgown down past her shoulders until it rumpled around her waist. She straightened slightly above him and he lifted his head to touch his tongue to one tight, dusky peak and his fingers to the other.

Meri arched her spine, welcoming more. His tongue circled and stroked each nipple in turn. Easing her forward, he gave more and more until her hips began to move against his and her fingers furrowed into his hair.

Breathing in familiar, arousing scents of leather and bergamot, Meri rose over Brew again. His black jacket and hair made a stark contrast to her flower-sprigged sheets; his white T-shirt looked almost golden in the candle's warm glow. He looked vital and masculine in her bed—a wild male only temporarily tamed.

Meri's heart pounded beneath her kiss-swollen breasts. With his patient loving, Brew was making her feel things she'd never felt—that she belonged with him for life, and that her love was reaching deep into him to touch him where no one's love had ever touched him before.

Wordless, she reached down to help him push his jacket off and pull his T-shirt over his head. She needed no prompting to thread her fingertips through his chest hair. Then she touched his nipples.

"You like that," she murmured, remembering the moonlit night on the hilltop.

"I *love* that," he drawled.

She bent to suck him as he had her. "And that?"

"That, too." His appreciative sigh was long and raspy. He caught her hair in his hand. "You didn't do that on page thirty-two."

"I'm rewriting, Brew."

"Don't rewrite the next page. I'm looking forward to that part."

Remembering what she had written, Meri blushed. "You don't have to . . . do that part."

"I do if I'm making your dreams come true." He grazed his palms over her breasts. "Not your nightmares but your dreams. They're my dreams, too." His mouth quirked in a sudden, crooked grin. "I've made dream love to you that would curl rose petals."

"Brew . . ."

He gathered her close and pillowed her head on his chest. "I *want* to do what you wrote. You'll never hear me say no to a long, slow taste of you."

Meri felt his hands glide under her nightgown and around over the cheeks of her bare bottom. He eased her onto her side with him and drew the gown lower until it was off altogether. Her first instinct was to press her thighs together and conceal herself from his frank, heated gaze.

"I know you won't hurt me, Brew, but it's been such a long time."

He nodded, caressing the curve of her hip. "I can wait." He brushed his knuckles whisper-lightly around the hollow of her navel and over the slight swell of her belly, then trailed them up between her breasts. "You're so beautiful I could just look all night," he assured her.

Bending his head again, he sucked gently on her nipple. She gasped. Where she hadn't been able to bear the thought of being touched before, Meri now craved Brew's touch. His gentle, generous lovemaking was breaching the barriers of fear. She knew he would take care of her. Head falling back, eyes closed, she opened to him.

Brew's fingers inched their way down her body yet again, this time to where he found her soft and throbbing, wet and wanting.

Meri sank farther back into her banked pillows as Brew stroked and caressed her. She began to move with him as he continued to arouse her with deft fingers. When she began to breathe in rhythm with his movements, she felt his body shift lower between her thighs. He kissed his way down from her breasts to her belly. Then his mouth joined in the slow, sure strokes that drew her hips to rise and fall.

Surprised, impassioned sounds slipped through her parted lips. Brew's hair slipped through her flexing fingers. Each rhythmic gliding, and circling of his tongue made her shudder, each time more frantically, until sensation burst and overflowed in joyous cries, as she climaxed.

Brew stretched out beside her again, holding her and savoring her surprised satisfaction. This, he knew, she could never forget—*would* never forget. He was breathless from her response.

"Brew..." she murmured wonderingly, then, "Brew..." once more before tears filled her eyes. "I've never been so . . . or had such a . . ." Unable to find the right words, she traced her fingers over his fantastic lips to convey that he'd been simply awesome. He'd made a dream true for her.

He replied by tasting each of her five fingertips. "Me and my smart mouth," he quipped. "It's finally doing me some good with you."

"You've done me more good than I can ever thank you for." Meri sighed. Secure in the circle of his arms, basking in exquisite sensations, she slipped open the top button of his jeans.

He touched her hand. "No thanks needed, Meri. Nothing."

"Not even the love I feel for you right now?" She freed the second button. "Don't you want to feel pleasure, too?"

"Not if it might remind you of being hurt."

She released the third button, watching the wedge of his fly widen. She chose her next words carefully, wanting to preserve the mood. "My attacker held me down. If you don't mind, I can love you ... on top."

Brew reached into his pocket and drew out a condom. "Mind?" he asked, guiding her fingers to the fourth button. "Why would I mind?"

"Because it's our first time and you're a macho, dominant man."

"In any way you don't like, Meri?" He stopped her hand again.

She smiled. "I'm discovering I like having a strong, rough-cut man like you around. I've never been fiercely independent or able to go my own way, like you do, yet, I feel more myself with you."

"I need you, too, Meri. You're gentle. You smooth away my rough edges."

Meri dispensed with the last button and teased, "What about this rough edge?"

"Only if you're sure you're ready."

"You made me ready." Meri laid her hand over the open vee of his fly. His white knit briefs molded to his shape.

"Nothing comes off unless you take it off," he murmured. "You want to just touch, touch. You want to just look, look. You haven't written this part yet."

"I'm writing it now, Brew." Meri slid her hand under the elastic of his briefs and touched him very tentatively. There she could feel every beat of Brew's heart.

She smiled and nestled her hand down lower.

Seeing her smile, Brew inquired, "Having fun, or *making* fun?"

"Having. I was so afraid it wouldn't be this easy."

"*I* was afraid this is where you'd start getting nervous."

"I am, a little," she admitted. "You are powerful, you know."

"For your pleasure only." His fingers stole between her thighs again. Caressing her distracted him from the tempting exploration she was conducting. It also made him want to thrust into her. But not yet. He closed his eyes.

"Keep that up and I'll never get your jeans off." She sighed, edging away. "I do want them off, Brew."

He lifted his hips to help her and there was the lengthy, sliding feeling of his jeans and briefs being pulled down his legs. Then he was completely naked. And she was silent.

He relaxed when he felt her begin tracing with one fingertip on his lower abdomen: his only tattoo had finally come to light. It consisted of three letters—*TNT*—each red, bordered in black.

"I used to think I was a real stud," he explained, his eyes still closed. He'd never felt so exposed. She might be turned off by the tattoo. She might pull back now, remembering the male body that had been an instrument of pain four years ago. She might be thinking all sorts of things—good or bad. "Say something, Meri."

"TNT," she said tracing each letter again. "Tough 'n' Tender. That's you."

He looked at her, then. Saw her slender hand return to him, her graceful fingers curl around his erection. He'd been fighting for control until now. He had to fight doubly hard when she held her other hand out for the condom.

"I know how," she reassured him, but her fingers shook in anticipation as she rolled it down on him.

Her lingering doubts were quickly dissipating as passion flared again deep inside her. She rose and knelt over him, then bent to kiss his mouth as she guided him with her hands.

Brew's indrawn breath hissed through his teeth. He felt only the slightest hesitation before she took him into her. "I'm so close, Meri—give me a minute." He clasped her hands tightly. "Don't move just yet."

Meri marveled at how easily, how eagerly her body had received him. She marveled more at realizing her power over him. He was giving her more than patience. He was giving her control. She knew that he could reverse positions and overpower her in one swift move. He could; but he wouldn't.

She lay very still upon him and said, "Tell me when."

"I will." He stroked her back and the curves of her bottom. To be held inside Meri was incredible. He rocked gently under her. "You tell me how you feel."

"Filled. Aroused."

"Nothing hurts? It feels good, the way it should?"

"It's never felt as good as this before. Truly."

Soon, guided by his hands on her hips, she began to move. Her mouth found his, and soft female whimpers mingled with harsh male sighs. The thick, crisp hair on his chest rubbed her nipples. The thicker, crisper hair at his groin tantalized her with every stroke. Their hunger and need intensified, their rhythm grew quicker, more urgent.

"Meri?"

"Yes—*yes*, Brew."

Then came the deepest probe, the softest gasp, a final thrust that brought them to the ecstasy of shared surrender.

"I'M HEAVY," Meri murmured much later, her lips moving against Brew's throat.

"You're a lightweight," he disagreed. "We could sleep like this if we wanted to."

"We can't tonight, Brew."

"When? Soon? I want longer than this with you."

"Brew, we have children. Remember?"

He nodded, smiled. "Yeah." At the thought of Meri giving birth to Trina, he hugged her more tightly to him. A sense of wonder filled him at the miracle of conception and birth.

"Brew, since Shannon has school every day, and Trina has preschool every day, could you take time off from work here and there this week?"

He grinned. "For the long, long lunches I'm already thinking about?"

"Could you?"

"I have a lot of time off coming. Shannon can sit Trina, too, a couple of nights this week. I'll pay. She needs the money after buying that dress." He stroked Meri's lower lip with the pad of his thumb. "And I sure need every minute I can get with you like this."

"Come tomorrow for lunch, then."

"I'll bring it," he promised.

12

BREW ARRIVED AT Meri's door five minutes after she got home from leaving Trina at pre-school.

"God, I've missed you," he said, locking the door behind him. He set the brown paper bag of Chinese takeout on the floor and pulled Meri into his arms for a long, deep thorough kiss.

She came into his embrace as she had never come before—with no reluctance, no hesitancy—and was breathless when she realized the change in herself. The dark burden of past memories had lifted. What freedom!

She opened her mouth eagerly to his kiss, needy and giving at the same time. She felt giddy and even a little out of control with desire. He was her lover—the man with the "slow hand" and the patience she had needed to feel normal again. He was joining her for a long, long lunch.

"I've missed you, too, Brew. You can't imagine."

"Yes, I can." He cupped her hips and held them against him. "Feel that? Damn good thing the lab coat I wear at work hid it all morning. Women have it made. They don't show what they're missing."

Meri twined her arms around his neck. "I couldn't sleep last night after you left. I wanted you with me."

"You want me now, too?"

"Yes."

"Before lunch?" he teased. "You think *you* got no sleep after I left? You should have seen me."

"I was trying to picture you, but I've never seen your bedroom."

"Show me yours again."

Hand in hand, they almost ran to her bedroom. She couldn't take his clothes off fast enough. His boots went thumping to the floor. His keys and loose change went spilling out of his jeans pockets.

Undressed, he fell back on the bed, taking her with him. He was so hard that he was almost embarrassed. Meri wasn't. She was touched.

"You want me this much, Brew?"

"I've never wanted a woman as much as I want you. Love makes a difference. I didn't know that until now."

"I did, but I've never known as wonderful a lover as you. Last night was just amazing for me."

"I took it easy enough, I hope?"

"You were everything I needed. I know what it cost you to take it easy, Brew."

"It was worth any price. I can be a bad boy in bed, for sure, but..." His words ended as his mouth caressed her breast.

Meri sighed. "Will you be that way with me someday?"

"Would it thrill you?" he whispered, moving his mouth lower.

"Yes." Meri half closed her eyes and floated on sensation. His hair was so dark against her white skin in the clear light of high noon. "The bad boy in you has always thrilled me." He was silent.

"Brew, say something."

He replied silently, first with his moist, hot breath between her legs, then with his nipping lips, finally with the fluttering tip of his tongue.

Meri was soon moaning, tossing her head from side to side, giving Brew total, loving access. And it was only the beginning.

SHANNON VOLUNTEERED to baby-sit Trina on Saturday afternoon, freeing Meri and Brew for a bike ride up to the hilltop. Still, there never seemed to be enough time or togetherness. Brew had work, school, and family time to share with Shannon. Meri had caring for Trina and work on her thesis to juggle.

In their few hours together, Meri had lain in Brew's arms telling him about her constricted life as a Mansfield. In turn, he'd told her more of his troubled years as a boy, and his undisciplined life as a young man.

"Would you ever think about marrying me?" he quietly asked on Monday.

"I've already thought about it, Brew."

"And . . . ?"

"Gran would be very difficult to bring around to the idea—perhaps even impossible."

"When does she come back from Boston?"

"This Thursday." So soon. Too soon. "I'll have to tell her about you."

"Tell her what?"

"That I love you. That my relationship with you is serious and might lead to marriage. She won't be happy to hear that."

"Because of who I am and who I've been, you mean. I'd be some grandson-in-law for her to swallow even if I cut my hair and wore a business suit to work."

"It wouldn't be as difficult if I didn't owe her so much," Meri explained. "Her moral code is Bostonian and strict, yes, but not unkind. She took me in and brought me up. My education was never less than the best. She also accepted Trina as a Mansfield despite who Trina's father was."

"Would you be here with me now if she was home?"

"Brew, don't ask me such questions. I wrestle enough with them myself."

"You wrestle *with* yourself, if you ask me. It's all up to you, Meri, not her."

"Nothing has ever been all up to me. A Mansfield's life is never completely her own to live."

"Who says? That's the way you want life to be for Trina? Living by someone else's set of rules?"

"No, but—"

"What's going to make it different if you don't make your own rules and choices?"

"Let's not discuss it until after I've told Gran what's been happening. You and I have been acquainted only a month. We may change our minds about each other in time."

"We've changed each other's lives in a month. I'm not the man I was a month ago and you're not the woman you were then." He grinned to make Meri stop from being so serious—and hopeless. "Look at how you're all over me right now. Look at the shape I'm in."

Sprawled on Brew in naked, shameless abandon, Meri couldn't deny anything he was saying. Relaxing into his teasing mood, she pressed her fingers to his nipples.

"Brew, I wouldn't doubt that you've always been in good shape in bed."

"I've never let anyone down," he acknowledged. "But I wasn't like I am with you. I didn't stick around to talk afterward, or even eat lunch. You, though, I could talk with all day."

Meri couldn't resist teasing, "So that's my great charm, is it? Talk?"

"Damn right. Action isn't all you want from *me*, is it?"

"Certainly not. However . . ." She sprawled more suggestively upon him, enjoying every aroused aspect of his hard body. "It's about all I can think about right now."

"Me, too, babe. Me, too."

She reached for a condom and made him ready. But this time, for the first time, she moved onto her back and invited, "Take me. Make me yours."

"Meri . . . Are you sure?"

"You've made me sure." She drew him down onto her body and between her legs.

Brew saw complete trust in her expression. He saw welcome and eager need. He saw her eyelids widen slightly at the first pressure. Restraining the urge to thrust, he probed gently all the way in.

"Ohhh. How good it is, Brew."

Brew knew she was his, then; entirely his. He gazed down into her eyes and saw the tremble of happy tears in them. There were tears in his own.

Her knees rose, her whisper coaxed, "Deeper." Wrapping her legs around his lean hips, she encouraged the hard thrusts he'd withheld for so long.

He responded by driving deep, lured by the pressure of her ankles against the small of his back. Under him she began to writhe, caught up in the unmistakable approach of release. He fought his own, waiting for ecstasy to engulf her before it took him.

Suddenly her racing heartbeat was his, her cries of climax all his. Swept away by the sound, he sank his deepest, truest thrust and let go with a shout of wild, unfettered triumph.

THE NEXT MORNING, Meri arranged an appointment for Shannon with the assessment office at her high school. Once the testing was complete, the evaluation would take a few weeks.

After marking Shannon's test day on the calendar, Meri stared at the date on which she'd written "Gran returns." How was she going to tell Gran what Gran didn't want to hear?

As Meri pondered that problem, Trina skipped into her office asking, "Can Brew be my daddy, Mommy?"

"Who gave you that idea, Trina?"

"Nobody. I thought it in my head."

"You already have a daddy, sweetheart." Meri's shoulders slumped with the lie. "He's far, far away in England, remember?"

"I want Brew, Mommy. He's not far, far away."

Meri shuddered, imagining Trina saying such things to Matilda. Nevertheless, muzzling a three-year-old was impossible. Meri knew she'd have to tell all about Brew before Trina presented Gran with requests for more than a puppy. She'd never dreaded anything as much.

Until then, though, there were yet more ways of loving Brew to explore than since the last time. She'd never looked forward to anything as much.

As ALWAYS, MATILDA'S homecoming was something of an event. She invariably brought gifts for everyone, including the servants.

For Santiago, a Spanish edition of *Larousse Gastronomique*. For Ingrid and Lars, gourmet smoked salmon. For Trina, an Easy Bunny picture book in advance of Easter Sunday, three days away. For Meri, a tooled-leather thesis cover.

"How about tea together at two tomorrow, Merideth?" Gran said after the gifts had been distributed and the servants were back at work. "We have catching up to do."

"Yes, Gran. We do."

She trudged back to the carriage house with Trina dancing alongside her, clutching the bunny book. The phone was ringing when they got inside. It was Brew calling from the San Jose pub.

"I just wanted to hear your voice," he said. "Why doesn't it sound like you're happy I called?"

"Gran is home. I'm having tea with her early tomorrow afternoon."

"And not looking forward to it, I hear. Want me to go with you?"

"As much as I'd love your support, it's best if I tell her alone."

"Okay. I'll come over around four to see how it went."

"No, Brew." Meri clutched the phone to her ear as if he were already on his way. "Don't do anything until I call you."

"You stick to your guns, Meri. If she throws you out on your ear, we'll get a place together. You, Trina, Shannon and yours truly—the Brodrick bunch."

"I'll call you, Brew."

"You do that. I'll be at the new pub in Berkeley."

"LEMON IN YOUR TEA TODAY, Merideth?" Matilda inquired at five minutes past two, the next afternoon.

"Yes, please, Gran." Meri was glad for one thing: Sunshine was pouring into the solarium today. It cheered, at least on the surface, as did the big pots of yellow tulips massed around the wicker chairs. Matilda was pouring tea from a china pot. Sunday tea, however, was always served in the tapestry-hung drawing room. The tea service used then was silver.

"Mind you, I'm not overly fond of Earl Grey," Matilda commented, passing Meri a cup, "but I know that you have a marked preference for the flavor." Matilda sat back with her own cup and saucer. "Now, then. Tell me what I missed in my absence."

Meri felt words sticking in her throat, refusing to come out. A sip of tea didn't help. The fragrance only reminded her of Brew and how impossible it had begun to seem that she'd become so intimately involved with him. Had marriage really been discussed as a serious possibility? Had she really thought until now that she could stick to her guns with Matilda Mansfield?

"I . . . Tell me what *I* missed in Boston," she hedged.

"I told you on the telephone every third evening when I called, Merideth. Dear old Beantown is not—and never will be, poor dear—San Francisco. It hasn't the same pizzazz, I'm afraid. How is Katrina doing at her little preschool?"

"Fine." Meri sipped again.

"And has Emmett set a wedding date? I don't believe you said when I last phoned."

"It's planned for late June, after school is out."

Matilda stirred her tea and set the spoon down. In a reproachingly inquisitive tone well-known to Meri, she remarked, "Ingrid tells me that Elsa stayed on one evening to sit Katrina. Emmett's student, I understand, needed assistance."

"Elsa was very kind to stay," Meri said. "Mr. Brodrick—er, Brew, as he's nicknamed—had some catching up to do before resuming his studies with Emmett."

Matilda's eyebrows rose. "Brew is a *nick*name?"

"Yes." Meri took a deep breath and set her cup and saucer down before they could start rattling in her hands. "He's the head brewer for three very reputable pubs here in the Bay Area."

"Elsa is apparently of the vulgar opinion that the man is a 'hunk,' to be precise," Matilda said. "I don't recall you describing him as such."

"I knew you wouldn't approve of anything about him," Meri ventured. "Just as you didn't approve of him in your first phone call from Boston. Actually, I've been seeing more of him than I've ever mentioned."

"While I've been away, Merideth?"

"I've fallen in love with him, Gran."

Matilda looked dumbstruck for a moment before rising from her chair, conscious as always that servants have big ears. "Come upstairs with me, Merideth."

Meri dutifully followed to her grandmother's bedroom suite.

"You can't be serious, miss," Matilda immediately declared when they were seated behind closed doors in her chintz-upholstered sitting room. "An uneducated beer brewer who lives among greasy motorcycles and an overpopulation of dogs is not a fit mate for a Mansfield."

"Gran, he happens to be improving his education in Emmett's classes. His two occupations and his living quarters aren't character faults. However, he's had many former faults that he has rectified."

"Such as?"

Gathering the very bare shreds of her courage, Meri told Brew's hard-edged story as she knew it. She glossed over nothing with regard to Tessa and Shannon, or

Brew's prison term. What should have been a joy to tell about her love for Brew and Shannon was as painful to reveal as it was necessary.

When it was all told, Matilda sat stone still, her expression horrified. "Can you even begin to imagine what the news reports would have to say about this man in relation to you?" she croaked. "We are Mansfields, Merideth—a name as prominent in this country as Vanderbilt and Rockefeller! Name one of them who has ever been involved with jailbirds and Devil's Advocates."

"Brew isn't a member of a bike gang, Gran."

"Neither are you a member of the middle or lower classes, Merideth."

"My father—"

"Your father was the only scandal our family tradition will ever suffer."

"He was the only *known* scandal," Meri countered. "I have an illegitimate daughter. Or have you forgotten?"

"You have a Mansfield. Whatever Katrina's paternity, she has Mansfield blood."

"If my attacker had been of a different race, Gran, you wouldn't be saying that. I wouldn't have a child now if that had been the case. You would have ordered an abortion or an adoption and covered *that* up."

"Only for the sake of the family would I have weighed my conscience with decisions of that sort."

"I want to continue seeing Brew, Gran. Let the news reporters have their moment. It won't be news for long. My 'marriage and divorce' certainly weren't."

"Modern society is accustomed to such news, Merideth. Think of the effect this story you've told will have on Katrina at her young age. Think of me and every good Mansfield in this good land. Your father's death will be dredged up and his estrangement from the family brought to light again. His unfortunate marriage, your lost-soul mother—everything will bear scrutiny."

"But, Gran, I'm such a minor member of the Mansfield family. I have no inheritance. I've never made waves, never been prominent or sought the limelight."

"You would have withered in its glare if your rape or Trina's illegitimacy had been made public knowledge. Your own poor judgment in tutoring that boy alone in a classroom at night would have been pointed up in every news headline."

Shaking, Meri stood. "My poor judgment didn't rape me. A rapist did!"

"Sit down and listen to me," Matilda snapped, waiting until Meri obeyed before continuing. "Your faulty judgment was a contributing factor. If you persist in applying it to your present situation with this beer brewer and his bastard daughter, your reputation will be destroyed. Your daughter's reputation will be at risk. What will she have as her stepfather, I ask you, if you are so unwise as to marry him? A man she can be proud of and look up to every day of her life? No. I think not."

"Gran, if *I* can be proud of the changes he's made in his life, Trina can. I'm not saying it won't be difficult and complicated, but—"

Matilda held up an unyielding hand. "Consequences of poor judgment can reach further than news headlines," she warned. "I disinherited your father without a cent before his death. Remember that."

"Had you accepted him instead, he and my mother might have been here having Sunday tea instead of surfing on Sunday afternoon," Meri retorted. "And if you hadn't drummed into me what good deeds Mansfields always do, I would have been the novelist I want to be. I wouldn't have been doing public service as a teacher and getting raped for it!"

Outraged, Matilda came to the edge of her chair. "How dare you charge me with such failings? You, who have lived on my charity from the age of six months to the day you began earning in your career!"

Charity. Meri felt her courage weaken under the singular weight of that word. A better one couldn't have been chosen to undermine a mutiny.

"I— Gran, I'm grateful, you know that."

"Have you no loyalty to me, the only parent you've ever known? No indebtedness for the years of care and concern I have wholeheartedly given you?"

Loyalty. Indebtedness. Charity. The combined effect of those oft-repeated words dragged Meri's high hopes down still further. She saw tears in Gran's eyes and recalled Grandad's funeral, the only time she'd seen Gran cry.

"You've been central to my life, Gran." More than central, Gran had been essential. Torn between Gran and Brew—the known and the unknown—Meri couldn't resist the stronger pull of every good thing

Gran had done for her. "I've never felt less than indebted or loyal to you."

"Demonstrate it, then, by ceasing and desisting from this brewer foolishness. Consider that there are greater consequences than scandal for ungrateful behavior. Wealth and power have been known to remove children from unfit parents and circumstances."

"You would . . . ?"

"My wealth and power have protected you and Katrina from even the slightest whisper of rape and illegitimacy, haven't they?" Matilda reminded, her tone brisk and without menace, but rich in implication.

Silenced by the possibility that Matilda could legally question her fitness as a parent, Meri sank slowly back in her chair. Losing custody of Trina would be devastating. It was unthinkable. *Trina, the light of my life.*

Would Gran go that far? Gran had disowned her son. She had already demonstrated her iron will when it came to closing ranks and maintaining the social order.

I have a will of my own, now that I've regained my self-esteem, Meri thought. *I'm adult and mature. I can survive without Gran. Trina and I would miss her terribly, though, if we were cut off. And where would that leave Gran, except alone with her empty pride?*

Trina's future might be at stake. Gran's happiness certainly was. Looking at Gran, Meri felt a pang of empathy. She saw more than an iron-willed adversary wielding a veiled threat; she saw a desperate old woman whose estranged son had died tragically, a widow without children of her own, a woman in the final years of her life.

"Very well," she brokenly agreed. "As you wish, I'll cease and desist, Gran."

Matilda nodded in satisfaction. "And we shall now forget that this unfortunate conversation ever took place." She rose from her chair. "More tea?"

13

AFTER A STIFF, stilted second cup of tea with Matilda in the solarium, Meri escaped to the carriage house. Picking up the phone before her tears could spill out and overcome her, she dialed Brew at the Berkeley pub.

"Brew, I—"

"You told her?"

"Yes, but—"

"I'm outta here and on my way." He clicked off.

"Brew, wait!" Fingers frantic, Meri dialed the number again. The wrong number. Finally, she got it right. Someone answered. She asked for Brew.

"He just left," she was told. "He's outta here."

Fifteen minutes later, Meri heard TNT arrive. Two seconds after that, Brew walked in, ripping off his helmet.

"So? What's the score?" In Meri's tear-reddened eyes and the defeated slump of her shoulders, he saw the answer. "Aw, Meri. She'll get over it if you stick to your guns."

Meri eluded the move he made to take her in his arms. "Don't, Brew. Please."

"Okay, I won't." He stepped back. "Give it to me straight. Are we on or off?"

"Gran is immovable. She reminded me of so many difficulties I've been ignoring. Seeing you in the future will be impossible for me. I—"

Brew held up a hand. "If we're off, I don't need a postmortem."

"It's not as if I don't love you, Brew."

"Yeah, it's only as if you don't love me enough, Meri. Pretty much the story of my life." Mouth drawn tight in a bitter, defensive line, he jammed his helmet back on his head. "I never pegged you as a coward, but that's what you are."

Coward! Meri grabbed his arm. "No, Brew. I'm not knuckling under as I've done before. I'm certainly not being unthinkingly obedient. I've come a long way since we first met. Now I'm doing what's best for everyone, including you."

"The hell if any Mansfield knows what's best for Brew Brodrick, including you. You dropped me once. You're dropping me again. I'm clear on the concept. You're a coward, and—"

"No!"

"And I've been a fool!" He turned on his heel and walked out.

Meri couldn't allow herself to fall completely apart. She had to pick up Trina from preschool in a few minutes. *Coward.* She covered her ears, but Brew's accusation echoed in her consciousness. *Coward... Coward...*

THE ACCUSING WORD WAS still with her the next day. After dragging out of bed, eyes swollen from tears, she sat and stared at page one twenty-five of her thesis on the computer screen.

Brew was only half-right, she thought. Shielding Trina wasn't cowardly; he'd do the same for Shannon. But the thesis was a cowardly thing—not what she wanted to be writing. She wanted to write of everything she had felt, of all she was feeling right now. She wanted to write *Dark Brew* in its entirety. In romance fiction there were happy endings after the dark despair of heartbreak.

Now that she couldn't have her own happy ending, she could at least write a story with one and prove that she wasn't a coward with respect to her creative gift. Certainly courage would be required to submit the book to publishers and face possible rejection.

Seeing one way that she might partly redeem herself in her own eyes, Meri brought *Dark Brew* up on the screen. Her three chapters were unstructured scenes— a very small part of what should be a larger whole to form a real story. Where to begin? At the beginning.

MERI WROTE AND COMPLETED *Dark Brew* within the next thirty days. The book became the testimony of her love for Brew, and of her pain at losing him. It became evidence of a creative energy she had only hoped she might find in herself.

For a month she put everything but Trina on hold and gave the rest of her time to the book. Sleepless nights found her in her office. Every spare minute found her there. Her only social occasions were Sunday tea and a dinner with Emmett one night to meet Alison.

During that month, Matilda remarked once that the thesis was taking an extraordinary amount of time and effort. Meri's reply was, "You want it to be worthy of a Mansfield, don't you?" If Matilda had concerns after that, she didn't express them. Life, on the surface, went on as usual.

That was fine with Meri. She knew a day of reckoning would arrive about the thesis and she was prepared for it. If she couldn't have Brew, she was going to have *Dark Brew*. Matilda would see the time spent as time wasted, of course, but would also see the product of it as the lesser of two evils.

In the first feverish week, Meri sent an outline of *Dark Brew* to a romance publisher for consideration. In the third week, an editor there wrote asking to see the manuscript when it was complete.

On the triumphant day when Meri typed "The End" on page two-eighty, she received a phone call from Emmett.

"Did you get my invitations, Meri?"

"Yes, both of them. But I've been so buried in the, er, thesis, that it slipped my mind to respond in time to the graduation invitation. You *know* I'll be at your wedding."

"Will you be at the graduation tomorrow night?"

Meri twisted the phone cord around her finger. "I'm afraid not."

"The class will be disappointed. They thought you were a great substitute." Emmett was silent a moment. "Even Brew asked in a roundabout way if you were coming."

"I'm afraid I can't."

"What happened, Meri? He won't say. You won't say. He looks like hell when I see him. You looked the same when I last saw you. Shannon says she'll get grounded if she says a word."

"Did she have a good time at the prom with your nephew?"

"So good that they're going steady."

"How did her testing turn out, Emmett?"

"Her scores were off the charts in verbal skills. She'll be diverted into special classes next year."

Meri managed a smile. "I was right, then."

"I wish you'd come tomorrow night, Meri. You should receive your share of credit for everyone's success. They've all got plans. An opportunity recently arose for Brew to work out a part ownership in one of the pubs."

"That's wonderful. Please . . . tell him how happy I am for him."

"Why don't you tell him in person at graduation?"

"Emmett, what happened is very complicated."

"As in how and why you got pregnant with Trina was very complicated?"

"Yes. Aren't you glad now that you didn't marry me in name only as you once offered to do? Alison is a lovely woman, as perfect for you as you are for her."

"And you, Meri, are as lonely as my fiancée is lovely. Be there tomorrow night and see the man you've been missing so much. I'd bet my teaching certificate that he's just as lonely for you."

"I'm sorry, Emmett. Tell everyone hello for me."

THE FOLLOWING DAY, the closer evening approached, the more nervous Meri became. She took Trina up to the big house to play there under Ingrid's care.

Alone in her office, she printed out the inch-thick manuscript of the book she had finished. Tomorrow she would mail it to the editor.

Coward. Brew's accusation came back to her as she held the completed manuscript in her hands. This, at least, had not been a cowardly effort. She lovingly traced a fingertip under the title, *Dark Brew,* and under the pen name she had chosen, Taffy Curtis. Her mother's name was from the Gaelic for "loved one." Her father's derived from Old French for "the courteous."

Brew would be proud to see this in its finished state, she reflected. He had been the inspiration, the flawed-but-heroic man who lived up to what William Shakespeare had written in *Measure For Measure.*

They say best men are moulded out of faults,
And, for the most, become much more the better
For being a little bad.

Brew, of course, had been more than a little bad. He'd outgrown most of it, but had retained the best, sexiest aspects of his faults. What woman didn't want a dash of the rebel in her man? What romance reader didn't want more than a dash of it in a romance hero?

Looking at the manuscript, hefting its weight in her hands, remembering every word she had fashioned her story from, Meri felt true courage fill her for the first time in her life.

All on her own, she had done it!

Dark Brew, like Trina, was hers and no one else's. Its happy ending, however, was not hers. At the end, her hero and heroine overcame every obstacle to their love and pledged their commitment to each other.

With Brew no longer in her life, Meri had no hero. A courageous heroine without a hero was not the stuff of romantic fantasy. Still, courage continued to fill her.

As it began to truly surge through her veins, she felt an impulse to bravely sweep up to the big house and tell Gran that she had just decided *not* to "cease and desist." That Brew and Shannon most certainly *would* be in-laws and welcome at Sunday tea. That Gran would have to fight a savage adversary if she tried to take Trina away. That the newspapers could say what they wished.

Fueled by the strength she had discovered in herself, Meri picked up a pen and wrote, "Happy Graduation, Brew. I love you," on the title page. Looking at it, she knew she had to go to his graduation. She had to give this to him and tell him—

Tell him what? That she was brave enough to write a book but not to live by her own rules? That she was too much a Mansfield to be a Brodrick? No. She would have to go with more bravery than writing the book had required. She would have to go prepared to be *everything* she wanted to be.

She smoothed a hand over the title page. If she had done this, she could do more. A feverish glance at the clock told her there was just time to slip into a dress and drive to the ceremony. She hurried to her closet to change, then tied a ribbon around the manuscript.

On the doorstep, she wavered and glanced over at the big house. Gran. She must be told. Now or later? Now. Mansfields never put off until tomorrow what they could do today.

Spurred by that thought, Meri marched up the flagstone path. Entering Matilda's immense kitchen, she waved to Santiago who was teaching Trina to knead bread. On through the big main hall she moved with conviction to the grand, curving staircase. Halfway up, she met Ingrid coming down.

"Mrs. Matilda is not feeling well," Ingrid said. "She wishes not to be disturbed."

"I wish to speak with her even so, Ingrid," Meri replied, continuing up the stairs. "Have Lars bring the sedan around, would you please?"

"But, Mrs. Matilda—"

"Gran is attending a high-school graduation tonight. It seems to have slipped her mind. Thank you, Ingrid."

"Yes, miss." Round-eyed, the housekeeper hurried down the stairs.

At Matilda's door, Meri knocked.

"I do *not* wish to be disturbed, Ingrid," she heard Matilda insist in a muffled voice.

"It's me, Gran. I must see you." Meri opened the door a crack. "Are you decent?"

"No, I am not decent."

Hearing her grandmother break off on a ragged sob, Meri entered the bedroom suite and found Matilda curled up, weeping, in one of the chintz chairs.

"Gran, what is it?" Meri knelt by the chair. "What's wrong?"

Matilda blew her nose on a lace-edged hankie. "*I* am what is wrong," she sniffed. "You were quite correct last month about my guilt in disinheriting your father. My accepting him would have saved his and your mother's life if he had been welcome at tea that Sunday."

"Oh, Gran. I didn't mean to—"

"You accused me of what I have known in my heart," Matilda sobbed. "Until now I refused to face it."

"Gran, don't cry. I was too harsh that day. I didn't realize you'd be so hurt by what I said."

"If I am, I deserve it, Merideth. You accused me of guilt in your being raped by that student. I'd never thought to blame myself. Now I do."

Meri stroked her grandmother's hand as fresh waves of tears soaked the hankie. Never had she seen Matilda like this—regretful, remorseful, self-doubting and repentant. Finally, Matilda calmed and blew her nose again.

"Have you truly always wished to be a novelist, Merideth?"

"Yes."

"And never said a word of it?"

"Would you have listened, Gran?"

Matilda took a deep breath. "No, I regret to say. Not until now. You would have been safe at your computer keyboard that ghastly night, writing away if I hadn't been such a tyrant."

"Gran, having Trina in my life more than made up for what happened to me. It was your wise guidance that led me to keep her rather than give her up to adoptive parents."

"I suppose I did do some good in that sense," Matilda allowed, wiping her eyes. "You know, I have never once thought of that child as anything but one-hundred-percent yours. And mine, too, through your father and you. I have no other links to him."

Meri took both of her grandmother's wrinkled hands in her own. "Perhaps you'll have more links through *me* one day."

"Not unless you marry and have children, Merideth."

"I intend to. Someday I will."

"I hope I live that long," Matilda said. "I see what I am and I loathe what I see."

"You're too upset to see the whole picture, Gran. It's never too late to change. I did—with Brew's help."

"Yes, I see a difference in you. Where do I begin? By giving Katrina the puppy she so badly wants? By acknowledging that your life is your own to live without my interference?"

"Those would be fine beginnings, Gran. You could attempt one more by coming to Brew's graduation right now."

"Brew." Matilda looked grim for a moment, then struggled to brighten. "If you love and trust him, I suppose he must be of good character."

Meri nodded. "Lars has the sedan waiting in the drive. I came up intending to tell you that you're going with me whether you like it or not. We both have amends to make to Brew."

"You had to be expecting I would object to being ordered to go anywhere."

"As far as I was concerned, Gran, you were going. I've made up my mind, whether you like it or not. That is that."

"How very like me you sound right now. That *is* that, I daresay, although I don't yet have a good feeling about you and this Brew."

"*I* do, Gran. That's all that matters."

"Well, if it will prevent another tragedy, I won't stand in your way. I'll find Katrina just the right dog, as well. A very small one, if you don't mind."

"Not at all," Meri soothed. "One step at a time."

Matilda stood, dabbing at her nose. "I do hope we won't be late. Mansfields are always punctual."

"Yes." Meri smiled at Matilda's unconscious slip. *Two steps forward, one step back. The walk of life.*

"What is this you have with you? Your thesis?"

"Not quite. I'll explain on the way to the graduation."

14

CONTRARY TO MANSFIELD tradition, Meri, Trina and Matilda were late arriving at the graduation ceremony in the community-college auditorium.

They took seats in the back row just as Emmett handed Hector Chamorro his certificate and shook Hector's hand to loud applause. Brew's startled gaze turned her way, and Meri focused on him alone.

"The next graduate to receive a diploma," Emmett announced after Hector, "is Baxter 'Brew' Brodrick."

Meri saw love flash in Brew's eyes for an instant. Then his features hardened into stony indifference as he rose from his seat. Dressed in a dark suit and tie, he had never looked more uncomfortable to her.

"Except for his hair, he doesn't *look* like a Devil's Advocate," Matilda whispered, her eyes following Brew's progress to the podium as she applauded with the rest of the audience.

"Mommy, is that Brew?" Trina inquired out loud.

"Yes, sweetie," Meri murmured under her breath. "Isn't he handsome?"

"Where's his real clothes?" Trina wanted to know before Matilda hushed her.

"In Brew Brodrick," Emmett announced from the podium, "we have yet another success story. As his daughter Shannon can attest, he juggled three jobs while he earned his GED certificate. One as Shannon's father, one as a skilled craftsman and one as head brewer for three Bay Area brew pubs.

"Like everyone else here, his past is past, and higher education, if he finds time for it—is now an option rather than a closed door." Emmett shifted on his crutch to hand over the certificate. "Brew, congratulations. Say a few words."

Exchanging a handshake, Brew stepped to the microphone. "I'd like to thank my number-one job for being my kid and accepting me as her dad. She didn't get a prize in me, but I got one in her. Thanks to Emmett. Teachers don't come any cooler than Magnusson."

His eyes slid across Meri to Trina, then returned to Meri. "Merideth Whitworth helped, too. She knew a poet when she saw one. That's it. Thanks, everyone."

He left the podium to hearty applause, Meri's, the most enthusiastic. When Emmett next called Arlene Ainsworth's name, Meri realized that the recipients were accepting in reverse alphabetical order. The ceremony was almost over.

She sought to catch Brew's gaze, but he sat looking down at the rolled-up diploma in his hands. Willing him to look at her, she stared at him. He refused throughout Arlene's thanks, throughout Emmett's concluding remarks, throughout the final applause.

He was still refusing when the stage vacated and everyone began milling in the reception area. Meri and Trina were immediately surrounded by Charleston,

Hector and Mai, who oohed and aahed over how much Trina resembled Meri. Hector had a daughter the same age and soon the two girls were playing among the rows of seats.

Meri caught sight of Emmett chatting away with Matilda, introducing her to faculty and school administrators. Keeping Brew in sight was easier; he was taller than everyone else. But all he would turn to her was his back.

Suddenly a high, girlish shriek sounded. "Meri! You came!" Shannon elbowed in and gave her a hug. "Thanks a zillion times for setting up the tests."

"You're the one who scored off the charts, Shannon."

"Wow! Emmett said you weren't coming." Shannon pulled her aside and mumbled, "I was wondering why Brew was looking all stone-faced and weird. Now I see."

"I have to talk to him, Shannon."

"About getting back together?"

Meri nodded. "Is he . . . seeing anyone else?"

"Nope. I'd know because I check his jacket pockets when he's not watching." Shannon raised an eyebrow, looking very wise. "Someone's gotta keep an eye on him until he finds himself a wife." Looking over Meri's shoulder, Shannon's eyes widened. She let out another shriek. "Munchkin!"

Instantly abandoned in favor of Trina, Meri pushed through the crowd to Brew who was comparing certificates with Charleston. She waited until Charleston melted away, then tugged on Brew's sleeve.

"Yeah?" Brew turned. His smile froze. "Oh. I thought you weren't coming."

"I got brave and decided you should have the first copy of my first book." She placed the ribbon-bound manuscript in his hands. "Not entirely a coward, Brew. A publisher wants to see it. I have a feeling it's going to sell."

"Whoa," he said, his cheekbones tinting as he read the title and her inscription. "When did this happen?"

"It began with you and ended with the last word, yesterday. A happy ending, actually."

He looked up from his graduation gift, his expression wary but softening. "You mean this? You love me?"

"I never stopped, Brew. I was wrong to send you away."

"Walking away was the toughest thing I've ever done."

"I hope to spend a lifetime making it up to you. Please try again with me."

"Are you standing on your own now?"

Meri pointed to her feet. "Count them. My own two feet. They're not toeing the Mansfield line. I *made* Gran come here, and wouldn't take no for an answer. Will you give me one last chance?"

He said nothing for so long that Meri thought all was lost. Then he looked up, into her eyes.

"Sure," he said, breaking into a bad-boy grin. "I'll even show you my tattoo."

"TNT—I can hardly wait!"

Meri stepped into Brew's embrace and lifted her lips to his kiss. This liberating moment was theirs, together.

She heard whistles, applause, and Trina exclaiming, "Mommy! Brew!" Gran's eyebrows were probably rising as high as they'd go. *Let them.*

It wasn't as if everything ahead would be easy. But to have her Brew at Sunday tea would be worth it.

A Note from Roseanne Williams

All my Temptation editor had to say was "bad boy," and I was *inspired*. Moody, dangerous and disreputable, Brew Brodrick roared into my mind on his sleek, black bike.

He was someone I knew well. A troublemaker, he had gone to grammar school with me. When he walked me down the aisle at our eighth-grade graduation, only my diary knew that I—the class valedictorian—was just crazy about the baddest boy in school. In high school, he became the sexy, rude-dude dropout all good girls dream of being bad with—just once in their ladylike lives. Only in their dreams.... Years later, as a high school teacher, I faced his teenage clone in my English class. He was the student from hell, disrupting my classroom, slashing my car tires, mocking school and society and me.

Yet the boy I first knew wasn't born to be wild. He came from a background of poverty, foster homes and never much love. I sensed that he yearned to be understood and accepted. He was street-smart and tough, but not invulnerable. His eyes used to meet mine and betray a tender streak, a sweet surprise. Down deep, he hungered to love and be loved.

My fond fantasy is that he grew up to be *The Bad Boy*, a Rebels & Rogues hero my Temptation readers could understand, accept and love with all their hearts. I'll always be just crazy about him. I hope you are, too.

HARLEQUIN Temptation

Rebels & Rogues

Quade had played by their rules...
now he was making his own.

The Patriot
by Lynn Michaels
Temptation #405, August

All men are not created equal. Some are rough
around the edges. Tough-minded but
tenderhearted. Incredibly sexy. The tempting
fulfillment of every woman's fantasy.

When it's time to fight for what they believe in, to
win that special woman, our Rebels and Rogues are
heroes at heart. Twelve Rebels and Rogues, one
each month in 1992, only from Harlequin
Temptation. Don't miss the upcoming books by
our fabulous authors, including Ruth Jean Dale,
Janice Kaiser and Kelly Street.

WELCOME TO

The quintessential small town where everyone knows everybody else!

Finally, books that capture the pleasure of tuning in to your favorite TV show!

GREAT READING...GREAT SAVINGS...AND A FABULOUS FREE GIFT!

Each book set in Tyler is a self-contained love story; together, the twelve novels stitch the fabric of the community. The covers honor the old American tradition of quilting; each cover depicts a patch of the large Tyler quilt.

With Tyler you can receive a fabulous gift ABSOLUTELY FREE by collecting proofs-of-purchase found in each Tyler book. And use our special Tyler coupons to save on your next TYLER book purchase.

Join your friends at Tyler for the sixth book, SUNSHINE by Pat Warren, available in August.

When Janice Eber becomes a widow, does her husband's friend David provide more than just friendship?

If you missed *Whirlwind* (March), *Bright Hopes* (April), *Wisconsin Wedding* (May), *Monkey Wrench* (June) or *Blazing Star* (July) and would like to order them, send your name, address, zip or postal code, along with a check or money order for $3.99 (please do not send cash), plus 75¢ postage and handling ($1.00 in Canada) for each book ordered, payable to Harlequin Reader Service to:

In the U.S.	**In Canada**
3010 Walden Avenue	P.O. Box 609
P.O. Box 1325	Fort Erie, Ontario
Buffalo, NY 14269-1325	L2A 5X3

Please specify book title(s) with your order.
Canadian residents add applicable federal and provincial taxes.

JAYNE ANN KRENTZ

Dreams
Parts One & Two

The warrior died at her feet, his blood running out of the cave entrance and mingling with the waterfall. With his last breath he cursed the woman—told her that her spirit would remain chained in the cave forever until a child was created and born there....

So goes the ancient legend of the Chained Lady and the curse that bound her throughout the ages—until destiny brought Diana Prentice and Colby Savager together under the influence of forces beyond their understanding. Suddenly they were both haunted by dreams that linked past and present, while their waking hours were filled with danger. Only when Colby, Diana's modern-day warrior, learned to love, could those dark forces be vanquished. Only then could Diana set the Chained Lady free....

BIG SUMMER READ

Summer Reading At Its Best

In July, Harlequin and Silhouette bring readers the Big Summer Read Program. Heat up your summer with these four exciting new novels by top Harlequin and Silhouette authors.

SOMEWHERE IN TIME by Barbara Bretton
YESTERDAY COMES TOMORROW by Rebecca Flanders
A DAY IN APRIL by Mary Lynn Baxter
LOVE CHILD by Patricia Coughlin

From time travel to fame and fortune, this program offers something for everyone.

Available at your favorite retail outlet.

BSR

HARLEQUIN
American Romance®

American Romance's year-long celebration continues. Join your favorite authors as they celebrate love set against the special times each month throughout 1992.

Next month, recall those sweet memories of summer love, of long, hot days . . . and even hotter nights in:

AUGUST

S	M	T	W	T	F	S
						1
2			6	7	8	
9			13			
16						
		25	26			

#449
OPPOSING CAMPS
by Judith Arnold

Read all the Calendar of Romance titles, coming to you one per month, all year, only in American Romance.